SUPERGRANNY

THE CASE OF THE
RIVERBOAT RIVERBELLE

Here they go again.

Supergranny, the Poindexter kids, Shackleford, and that spoiled but lovable robot, Chesterton, set out for a peaceful Mississippi riverboat cruise.

But the Twittle Twins, notorious bald, cigar-smoking crooks, have launched another plan — a fiendish crime complete with piracy, pig rustling and a mysterious island.

Can Supergranny and friends squelch the crime and squash the Twittles?

 printed on recycled paper

Supergranny Mysteries

Supergranny 1: The Mystery of the Shrunken Heads
ISBN 0-916761-16-9
Library Hardcover: ISBN 0-916761-17-7

Supergranny 2: The Case of The Riverboat Riverbelle
ISBN 0-916761-22-3
Library Hardcover: ISBN 0-916761-23-1

Supergranny 3: The Ghost of Heidelberg Castle
ISBN 0-916761-20-7
Library Hardcover: ISBN 0-916761-21-5

Supergranny 4: The Secret of Devil Mountain
ISBN 0-916761-04-5
Library Hardcover: ISBN 0-916761-05-3

Supergranny 5: The Character Who Came to Life
ISBN 0-916761-18-5
Library Hardcover: ISBN 0-916761-19-3

Supergranny 6: The Great College Caper
ISBN 0-916761-14-2
Library Hardcover: ISBN 0-916761-15-0

Buy Supergranny mysteries at your local bookstore, or ask the bookstore to order them. Or order them yourself with this coupon.

Holderby & Bierce, Publishing
3245 Halcyon Drive
Bettendorf, IA 52722

Please send the Supergranny mysteries checked above. Enclosed is my check or money order for $ _____ ($3.25 for each paperback, $9.95 for each hardcover; plus $1.50 postage and handling per order.)

Name _____

Address _____

City _____ State _____ Zip _____

Allow 2 weeks for delivery.
Prices subject to change and offer to withdrawal without notice.

SUPERGRANNY

THE CASE OF THE RIVERBOAT RIVERBELLE

Beverly Hennen Van Hook

Holderby & Bierce

Published by Holderby & Bierce, 3245 Halcyon Drive
Bettendorf, IA 52722

Andrea Nelken, editor

Paperback. ISBN 0-916761-22-3
Library Hardcover. ISBN 0-916761-23-1

SUMMARY: Second in the mystery series about Supergranny, an elderly detective who drives a red Ferrari and fights crime with the help of the three kids next door. A peaceful Mississippi River cruise turns into an adventure involving piracy, pig rustling and a mysterious island.

Holderby & Bierce, October, 1986
2nd Printing, March, 1987
3rd Printing, October, 1988
4th Printing, September, 1993

Printed in the U.S.A.

To Daddy

It was not one of our better mornings.

For one thing, it was raining.

For another, Supergranny thought she was coming down with the flu.

When I got to her kitchen about 9 o'clock there she was, totally wrapped in her rainbow afghan, propped up on the bench beside her fireplace. All you could see were her bifocals, the thermometer sticking out of her mouth and her hand holding a cardboard slate.

It was one of those slates where you pull up the plastic sheet to erase the message, and I groaned at the sight of it.

I knew what it meant — notes.

We had been through the slate business once before when Angela, Vannie and I had nursed Supergranny through a sore throat. Angela and Vannie are my older and younger sisters. We live right across the ravine from Supergranny, otherwise known as Sadie Geraldine Oglepop.

Anyway, from the sore throat ordeal, I knew the slate meant notes. Dozens of notes. Hundreds. Thousands. Maybe millions of notes.

Already, she was scribbling a note on the slate.

"TEA," it said.

I headed for the teakettle.

Thump, thump, thump, went the slate on the bench. That's how she gets your attention when she has a sore throat, or a thermometer in her mouth, or can't talk for some reason, or thinks she can't. She thumps things with the slate.

I turned to look at the slate she held up for me.

"PLEASE," it said.

"Sure, no problem," I said and started for the teakettle again.

Thump, thump, thump, went the slate.

See what I mean? The thumping gets old fast.

"I'll be right there," I said, and went ahead and filled the teakettle and set it on the stove.

She held up the slate as I sat down on the other bench beside the fireplace.

"WHERE'S AV?" it asked.

"AV" is her shorthand for Angela and Vannie.

"They'll be here in a minute," I said. "Angela is drying her hair, and Vannie can't leave the house until Mom can see at least 70 percent of her bedroom floor."

Vannie's room is an ongoing disaster. You can never see the carpet for all the junk on the floor.

Of course, Angela's room isn't perfect, either. There are usually a couple of desk drawers open and five or six library books and a hair dryer on the floor.

And even my room gets away from me sometimes, like when my beer can collection goes berserk and rolls all over the floor. Or when somebody drapes jeans and pajamas around.

But Vannie's room is in a class by itself.

It's an all-drawers-open-old-leg-warmers-broken-crayon-last-year's-math-paper-old-kindergarten-class-picture-coat-hanger-dried-raisin-box-bent-radio-antenna-stuffed Class Double A Disaster.

Angela says it looks like the Wreck of the Hesperus.

Supergranny says it looks like it has been stirred.

Dad says it looks like Vannie's floor is her closet.

Mom says, "Clean it up, clean it up, clean it up . . ."

But at that point, Vannie's room was the least of our worries. We had other problems to contend with. I took a quick look at my watch. We were due at the boat dock in less than an hour, and here Supergranny was all bundled up with the flu.

She caught me looking at my watch and tilted her head to glare around the thermometer at my wrist.

"Good night, look at the time!" she said, plucking the thermometer out of her mouth. "We'll be late, and Captain Tubweathers will have a conniption fit. She's counting on us."

She handed me the thermometer. "Joshua, read this thing while I pour the tea."

I turned the thermometer slowly in my fingers and squinted at the silver line of mercury. I'm new at thermometer reading and it takes me a while because the mercury keeps jumping around.

"Ninety-two?" I guessed.

"That's impossible, Joshua," said Angela, breezing in the door with Vannie. "It has to be more than that."

She grabbed the thermometer and held it at nose level. "Ninety-eight point six. Right on the arrow. Normal. Perfect," she said, shaking the thermometer briskly.

"Really?" Supergranny asked, sipping tea. "I thought it would be at least 102°. I feel terrible."

She sipped more tea and reconsidered. "That is, I *felt* terrible. I think I'm feeling better. Maybe it was one of those new, short flus. Or maybe it was my allergies."

"Or maybe it was the rain," Vannie suggested.

Supergranny is not crazy about daytime rain. She prefers nighttime rain so people can fall asleep to the sound of it on the roof. She says daytime rain gets in her way.

And she downright hates working on a riverboat in the rain, which is what we had to do that day. Just thinking about it can bring on flu symptoms. So her friends have to look on the bright side to help rev her up.

Angela started the revving.

"While I was drying my hair, I heard on the radio that the rain is supposed to stop," she said. "Sometime."

"It was slacking up when we came over," Vannie said. "A little."

"By the time we get aboard, the sun will be out," I said. "Maybe."

The words had hardly left my mouth when the rain

slammed the kitchen window with a mighty whoosh, then started coming down worse than ever.

Supergranny laughed.

It was a good sign. She was snapping out of it.

"Angela, get the snickerdoodles," she said.

The snickerdoodle cookies were in the safe behind the teapot-shaped wall clock. As Angela worked the combination, Supergranny folded the afghan and put it on the bench on top of the slate. It looked as if the slate weren't coming with us — another good sign. Maybe the day wouldn't turn out so bad after all.

The four of us stood in front of the fireplace, each munching a snickerdoodle. Then I pushed the yellow fireplace button.

Instantly, the fireplace divided down the middle and opened like sliding doors, and "Stars and Stripes Forever" boomed out of the ceiling.

We quickly crossed through the fireplace into Supergranny's workshop-office-laboratory-playroom-garage.

I've been inside Supergranny's office so many times by now that the shock has worn off. I mean, you just eat a snickerdoodle with the secret ingredient, push the yellow button, and, whammo, the fireplace doors open to the office. It's routine.

But you should have seen me that first day when we were just moving in from Cleveland. Little did I know what I was getting into when I'd come over looking for our Old English sheepdog, Shackleford, who had blundered out of our yard by mistake.

I mean, we had nice neighbors in Cleveland, but nobody had a secret room behind the fireplace. Or if they did, *I* never knew about it.

But shock or no shock, I still think Supergranny's office is about the best room in the world. I think you could look for 137 years and not find a better one.

There was the Ferrari, waiting to take us down to the river. And there was Chesterton, raring to go along.

Chesterton, of course, is Supergranny's pet robot. He's about the size of a loaf of bread and is fueled by gumdrops that you put in a coffee-cup-shaped sensor on top his head. He can be lots of fun . . . and lots of trouble. Sometimes he's more trouble than fun, if you ask me, but don't tell Supergranny. She has spoiled him rotten.

He wasn't about to let a little rain slow him down. He'd already dragged his Maine Lobsterman rain slicker out of the closet, and as soon as he saw us he started pestering Vannie to tie his rain hat strings.

In five minutes we were all in the Ferrari, ready to go. It was snug with the top up, and it was going to get snugger.

"First we stop by your house to pick up Shackleford," Supergranny said. "We don't dare go to the boat without her. Captain Tubweathers would keelhaul us."

At that, Angela pushed the button on the dashboard, the garage door opened, and we roared down the drive.

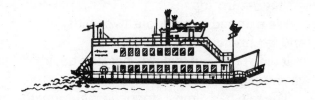

Thousands of bicycles with riders were swarming around the dock when we got to the river. A large banner, "WELCOME TO ROTRATTT," was stretched above the dock. It was the annual "Ride Over the River and Through the Town" day, better known as "ROTRATTT."

Our town straddles the Mississippi River, and every year there's this twenty-mile bike ride. People start at the baseball stadium, pedal upriver to the dock, and cross the Mississippi on Captain Tubweather's excursion boat. Then they disembark on the other side, ride their bikes downriver to the bridge, and cross the bridge back to the stadium.

The bikers pay an entry fee that goes to charity, and Supergranny works the ride as a volunteer each year. This was Angela, Vannie and my first year to help, although we had ridden on Captain Tubweather's Riverboat River-belle lots of times before.

As usual, we didn't realize what we were getting into.

We thought we'd just help 800 bikers wheel their bikes up the ramp onto the top deck, ride across the river, help the bikers off on the other side, then go up to the pilot house and play gin rummy on the return trip.

After the bikers leave, the boat is empty except for the crew, so Captain Tubweathers always hosts her annual ROTRATTT All Day Invitational Gin Rummy Tournament on the return trip.

We planned to work our two shifts, play a little rummy and go home.

It didn't turn out that way because about 537 things went wrong. But more about that later.

The rain had almost stopped when Supergranny parked the Ferrari. But the wet, gray sky merged with the wet, gray river, and you couldn't quite tell where sky stopped and river started.

For all our eyes knew, the Riverbelle, just now docking after delivering the first batch of bikers, could have been drifting right out of the gray sky. (Of course, our brains knew better.)

"Put these on," Supergranny said, handing us red ROT-RATTT CREW armbands. "Angela, you'd better put Chesterton in your tote. I don't want him getting lost in the crowd.

"Joshua, keep a firm hold on Shackleford's leash. She's so bashful she's likely to bolt when she sees all the people."

She was right. Shackleford is totally bashful. Clomping her way through a thousand strange bikes and bikers is *not* her idea of a good time.

But although she is leery of crowds, Shackleford loves riding on boats almost as much as she loves riding in cars.

So the thing to do was to keep her mind on the boat and off the bikers as much as possible.

"Boat, Shackleford," I whispered in her ear as we climbed out of the Ferrari.

"BOAT, SHACKLEFORD," Vannie yelled as we headed toward the crowd.

"BOAT, SHACKLEFORD; BOAT, SHACKLEFORD; BOAT, SHACKLEFORD," we all chanted, threading our way to the dock.

*   *   *   *   *   *

Captain Tubweathers kept the bikers behind a long chain while the first-shift crew left and we boarded. She is six feet tall and has a severe limp from a barge accident. She had worked river barges for thirty years to save enough money for the Riverboat *Riverbelle's* down payment.

She's usually such a jolly person that I was surprised at her worried look as we came up the gangplank.

"Thank heavens you're here, Sadie," she said to Supergranny. "Something terribly strange has happened. I must talk to you privately as soon as we unload the bikers on the other side."

Then she saw Shackleford and grinned. She has a soft spot for Shackleford, maybe because Shackleford is as goofy over the *Riverbelle* as she is.

"Welcome aboard, Shackleford," she said. "You come with me up to the pilot house out of the crowd. I don't

9

want you to be spooked by a 12-speed and fall overboard."

Then she gave the rest of us assignments, pointing at the narrow ramps that had been placed up the center of the stairs.

"Sadie, you and Vannie stand at the middle of the stairs on either side of the ramp.

"Angela and Joshua, you do the same at the bottom. When the bikers wheel their bikes up the ramp, Angela and Joshua will help them halfway up the ramp, then Sadie and Vannie will take over. At the top, my first mate Clarence will direct them to their parking spots.

"Does everybody know Clarence?" she asked.

We agreed that we all knew Clarence, a nice man but a cutthroat rummy player.

Clarence touched his cap in a casual salute and grinned. We knew why he was grinning. He was preparing to slaughter us at gin rummy.

*   *   *   *   *   *

Captain Tubweathers stood outside the pilot house and surveyed the crew. I could barely see the top of Shackleford's head above the railing beside her.

The air was quiet and still.

Supergranny, Vannie, Angela and I stood at our posts on the stairs. Second Mate stood at the gangplank, waiting for the signal to open the chain for the bikers.

Grinning Clarence stood at attention on the top deck.

Chesterton, still wearing his yellow rain cap, peeked over the edge of Angela's tote, which hung on the stairway railing.

10

I hoped he would stay put. Pushing 800 bikes up a ramp was going to keep us busy enough without worrying about Chesterton tripping a biker or diving into the Mississippi.

I followed Captain Tubweather's eyes around the brightly painted, red and white sternwheeler. It looked as fancy as a floating wedding cake — if they make red and white wedding cakes. Banners flew from gaily colored smokestacks, balloons danced from curved railings, and layers on layers of decks reached to the sky.

The Captain's worried look melted away as she surveyed it all, and she grinned as her eyes stopped at the crown jewel of the Riverboat Riverbelle.

It was Clyde the Crazy Steam Calliope with Mazie Mayberry at the keyboard. When Supergranny was a girl, tons of riverboats had calliopes, musical instruments that are sort of a cross between an organ and a steam-whistle convention.

But these days calliopes are so scarce, you're lucky if you've ever heard one. And if you've heard Mazie Mayberry play one, you're top-lottery-winner lucky as a calliope listener. Mazie is the best calliope player in the Midwest and possibly the known world.

With Mazie at the keys, Clyde the Crazy Calliope could laugh, cry, play the "Moonlight Sonata" and curse in three languages.

Captain Tubweathers swept her arm above her like a conductor at the podium. *Swoosh*, her imaginary baton cut the air.

At the signal, Second Mate dropped the gangplank chain, calliope music filled the air, and 800 helmeted bikers thundered toward us.

11

3

If you've ever been shanghaied into loading 800 bikes onto the top deck of a riverboat, you know the secret is to keep the bikes moving up the ramp.

The hitch comes when a biker gets to the top, then stops to admire the view or look around for the restroom.

This creates a bike jam and leaves you holding the next bike halfway up the ramp. As everyone knows, a bike standing at midramp is determined to do one and only one thing — roll backward and crash into the bike waiting at the bottom. And the sooner the better, as far as the bike is concerned.

Meanwhile, you've got to convince it not to do it.

Otherwise, the person at the bottom might crash into the person behind her, and the whole line might fall like dominoes clear back to the last person in line out on the pier.

Unlikely, true, but the sort of thing that flashes through your mind when you're the bike-holder on the ramp.

The longer the person at the top admires the view or looks around for the restroom, the more the bike insists on crashing backward. It's not so hard to hold Bike 347, say, but by the time you get to Bike 722 you don't care much anymore.

We had a few bikeslides, but, luckily, no damage, and we finally got them all aboard. In fact, we beat the first-shift crew's loading time by two minutes, which wasn't bad.

Supergranny, Angela, Vannie and I collapsed by the stern railing to compare notes. We had only fifteen minutes to rest before we had to help the bikers unload on the other bank.

"Rest while you've got the chance," Supergranny said, "because unloading is trickier than loading. People stop at the bottom to look around for their friends, and you get caught holding a bike going down-ramp."

"Great," I groaned. "Very encouraging."

"I'm just warning you," she went on. "A bike stopped facing *downhill* is ten times more bent on getting to the bottom than one facing *uphill*."

"It could be worse," Vannie said. "They could be riding camels."

"Or elephants." Angela laughed.

"Whisper when you say that," Supergranny said. "The Chamber of Commerce might hear you and sponsor an elephant ride."

"TGERR," Angela said. "The Great Elephant River Ride."

Of course, we were just joking. Working the boat was fun. ROTRATT was a good idea, and we were glad our town had it. Most of the bikers were great, even if a few did forget to keep moving at the top of the ramp.

They joked with us, thanked us at the top, and, except for a few real young kids, helped steer their bikes as we wheeled them up the ramp.

In fact, I could remember only two exceptions. Strange exceptions now that I had a chance to sit on the deck and think about them.

The first had been a stocky, middle-aged man of about 60 wearing a fluorescent orange sweat suit and a black helmet. He'd had a cream and orange bike. I remembered because I happened to grab the bike wrong and accidently pulled the tire pump loose.

"Klutz," he'd muttered, glaring at me and snatching the pump out of my hand.

The second had been near the end of the line. He was a stocky, middle-aged man of about 60 wearing a fluorescent orange sweat suit and a black helmet. He'd had a cream and orange bike.

When he started up the ramp, he had picked up his bike and brushed us aside. Picking up his bike wasn't unusual. Many people carried their bikes up. But it was the *way* he did it. Although he didn't actually speak, his manner seemed to say, "Don't touch my bike, peasants!"

"It's odd," I said. "The only two rude people out of all those bikers looked alike."

"You mean the older guys with the black helmets?" Angela asked.

"And the orange sweat suits?" Vannie asked.

"And the orange and cream bikes?" Supergranny asked.

"Yeah, yeah and yeah," I said. "Odd."

We all agreed that it was an odd coincidence, then forgot about it as we dragged ourselves to the stairway to help unload.

It was odd, all right. But as it turned out, it was no coincidence.

*　　　*　　　*　　　*　　　*　　　*

After the bikers unloaded, Captain Tubweathers and Second Mate could handle the Riverbelle themselves on the return trip.

The plan was for the rest of us — Clarence, Supergranny, Angela, Vannie and me — to play in the rummy tournament. Mazie, of course, would stick to playing calliope.

As soon as the last bike hit the gangplank, we all trooped up to the pilot house where Clarence had already dealt the first hand and was ready to skin us.

"Not yet, Clarence," Supergranny said. "Chesterton and Shackleford have to be attended to first."

Chesterton was moderately cross from being cooped up in Angela's tote, and I couldn't say I blamed him.

"Now that the bikers are gone, I think we can trust Chesterton on deck," Supergranny said. "Joshua, better take him for a walk around the boat to settle him down."

That meant Clarence had to re-deal, leaving me out of the first hand. He didn't like it much, but he did it.

Meanwhile, Shackleford, seeing that Chesterton was going for a walk, started begging to go, too.

"Angela, I guess you'd better take Shackleford for a turn around the deck, too," Supergranny said.

That meant Clarence had to re-deal again, leaving Angela out of the first hand. From the way he slapped down the cards as he dealt, you could tell he didn't like it.

"Sadie, let's have that private talk now, before we start back," Captain Tubweathers said. The two of them headed down to the galley.

That meant Clarence had to re-deal, leaving Supergranny out of the first hand. Now only he and Vannie were left. He gritted his teeth and dealt.

"Clarence, could you wait just a minute," I heard Vannie say as I went out on deck. "I have to go to the bathroom."

Poor Clarence. As I walked around the deck, I could see him through the pilot house window, throwing the cards in the air. He just kept picking them up and throwing them in the air, picking them up and throwing them in the air.

The reason we'd kept Chesterton bagged in the tote while the 800 bikers were aboard is that he tends to go hyper if there's too much excitement. I was worried that even with the deck to ourselves he'd get excited about a gull or something and scoot right under the railing into the drink, although Supergranny had bribed him not to.

"Mind Joshua and don't fall overboard, and I'll give

you some nice gumdrops when you get back," she had promised.

It worked at first. Then he got bored just walking and decided it would be more fun if I chased him instead.

Boom, he was off, dashing around the corner and down to the lower deck. I clattered after him, but by the time I got to the bottom he was gone.

The deck was completely empty.

Had he already made it around the corner to the starboard side?

Was he hiding in a storage closet?

Had he fallen overboard?

I looked overboard, half afraid I'd see him and half thinking it would serve him right. Chesterton is a good swimmer, but he rusts. As far as I could see, there weren't any small robots thrashing around in the waves, so I started checking out the storage closets. I started with the one farthest down the deck because its door was ajar.

No Chesterton. But there *was* something strange — an orange and cream bicycle.

Wait a minute, I thought. Everybody who came on had a bicycle and everybody who got off had a bicycle. So who does this bicycle belong to? Clarence, maybe? Captain Tubweathers? Second Mate?

Just then something streaked behind me and up the stairs. Chesterton, the peskiest robot in the Western world. I galloped after him up to the pilot house.

The others were just returning. Captain Tubweathers was already back at the wheel, and the boat was easing away from the dock.

17

"Shall I deal?" Clarence asked hopefully.

"Not yet, Clarence," Supergranny said solemnly. "Captain Tubweathers has a problem and she needs our help."

Just then Vannie came back from the restroom.

"Somebody forgot a bicycle," she said. "It's in the restroom."

"And there's one in a storage closet down below," I said.

Supergranny looked quickly at the Captain and mates. "Did any of you bring a bike on board?"

They shook their heads, looking puzzled.

Nobody said anything as the Riverbelle eased into the main channel. The fog had settled in again, thick as gauze.

"Everybody who boarded brought a bicycle except us," Supergranny said slowly. "Everybody who got off took a bicycle. That means . . ."

"Stowaways," Vannie whispered. "We've got two stowaways on board."

4

"We'll have to search the Riverbelle," Supergranny said. "But first, I want to brief everyone about the threats. OK, Captain?"

"Whatever you say, Sadie," Captain Tubweathers answered.

Supergranny sat on the edge of the formica-topped table that Clarence had moved up from the galley for the game. The rest of us gathered around, except for Captain, of course, who was at the wheel.

"Take a look at this," Supergranny said, passing around a sheet of lined yellow paper. Letters cut out from newspaper headlines were pasted on it.

"Stop RATROT," it said.

"RATROT?" Vannie asked. "They must mean ROT-RATTT."

"Obviously," Angela said. "Obviously" was Angela's new word of the week. She would pick a word, use it to death, then move on to a new one. Last week's had been "brilliant." The school assembly was "brilliant," Vannie's new tennis shoes were "brilliant," Stevie Wonder's new song was "incredibly brilliant." It was a relief to move on to "obviously."

"I found the note tucked inside my front door when I opened it to get the newspaper this morning," Captain said.

"I thought it was just some childish prank and didn't pay much attention. Then I got a threatening phone call while I was drinking my coffee. He said if I transported the bikes today, I'd never pilot the Riverbelle again."

"But why would anybody want to stop ROTRATTT?" I asked.

"Did you recognize the voice?" Angela asked.

"Are you sure it was a man?" Vannie asked.

Captain fielded the last question first.

"Yes, I'm pretty sure it was a man, Vannie, although he was trying to disguise his voice.

"As to the rest, I didn't recognize him, and I'm as baffled as you are about the motive. ROTRATTT is for charity. Why would anybody want to stop it? Even after the phone call, I thought it might be a crazy prank. But after what happened to the Riverbelle this morning, I'm not so sure."

"What happened to the Riverbelle?" I asked, remembering her worried look when we boarded.

"Battery cable," she said grimly. "Someone had cut clean through the Riverbelle's battery cable. The engine was as dead as frozen hamburger. Luckily, Second Mate and I were here early enough to fix it."

"But why?" Angela asked for the thirteenth time. "Why would anybody want to stop ROTRATTT?"

"The only person or persons who know the answer to that may hiding on this boat," Supergranny said grimly. "Our first job is to find him."

"Or them," Vannie said. "Him or them."

"Right," Supergranny said. She told Second Mate to stay with Captain and divided the rest of us into teams.

"Vannie, Chesterton and I will take the starboard side. Angela, Joshua and Shackleford take port. Clarence, you go up to the calliope and stick by Mazie."

"I guess that means I should put away the cards," Clarence said.

Supergranny sighed. "Yes, Clarence."

"Not even one little hand first, for luck?" Clarence asked.

Supergranny sighed again. "No, Clarence."

"One quick hand, to settle our nerves?" Clarence asked.

"PUT AWAY THE CARDS, CLARENCE," Supergranny said in her best chief executive officer voice. Supergranny doesn't use her chief executive officer voice much, but when she does, it gets results. Peter the Great would have put away the cards.

Clarence put away the cards.

"OK, we're already midchannel, so we've got only ten minutes to catch the culprit before we start pulling in to dock," Supergranny said.

"We'll use Plan 432B. I'll go over the details while Angela hands out the whistles." She always carries whistles along with certain other equipment in her purse. Always. She says in fighting crooks, whistles give you an edge.

Angela, Vannie and I had been over Plan 432B so many

times we could rattle it off like multiplication tables. But it took some doing to get it across to Clarence. He finally got the hang of it, or said he did.

I don't know what took him so long to catch on. We had to do all the work. All he had to do was stand beside Mazie and blow his whistle at the first sign of trouble. For some reason, though, he couldn't seem to get it through his head. He kept wanting to know what kind of trouble.

"Any kind of trouble," Supergranny said. "Don't worry, you'll know it when you see it."

Finally, we got him to go up to Mazie.

We left Captain and Second Mate in the pilot house and started to search the boat while Mazie played "Daisy, Daisy, Give Me Your Answer True." You know, that old song about "The Bicycle Built for Two."

Our two teams split up at the stern, and Angela, Shackleford and I started up the port side. By now the fog was so thick you couldn't see the bow of the Riverbelle. We worked our way slowly along the deck, checking all the storage closets, stairwells and restrooms along the way. By the time we met the other team at the bow, Mazie had played "Daisy" three times, and I was getting slightly sick of it.

It was a great relief when she switched to "Alley Cat."

Supergranny signaled from the other side of the bow that their team hadn't found anything either, and we all edged our way along the bicycle ramp down the stairs.

Reaching the lower deck, we split up again.

The lower deck was harder to search because of the "Grand Salon." That's a big enclosed room where people eat dinner on the regular Riverbelle dinner cruise and dance on the Saturday night dance cruise.

We had celebrated there on Mom's birthday.

That day it had been packed with people and laughter and white-coated waiters singing silly songs. We'd eaten roast beef, waved to the fishermen and walkers along the shore and teased Mom about getting old.

Now it was hard to believe this shadowy, cavernous room was the same Grand Salon. It was gloomy, quiet and empty.

At least, I hoped it was empty.

"Guard the door," Angela whispered as she and Shackleford slipped past me into the Salon. "I'll check behind the buffet, and Shackleford can sniff under the tables."

You can always count on Shackleford to sniff under dining room tables. To be honest, she was not really looking for stowaways, she was looking for crumbs. But, believe me, if she *had* bumped into a stowaway she would not have sniffed around him and gone on merrily looking for crumbs. She would have yelped, run, panicked and just generally let us know.

Angela was halfway to the buffet counter, and Shackleford was already under the second table when suddenly there was a noise on the other side of the room.

We froze.

The starboard door into the Grand Salon creaked open slowly, and a figure slipped inside.

It was Vannie. Shackleford took a break from under-the-table sniffing and ran noisily to greet her.

"Rats," Angela barked. "If we're going to be this obvious you might as well turn on the lights, Joshua."

Angela tends to get annoyed when things don't go according to plan. Plan 432B called for quiet; therefore, she thought we should be quiet. So did I, but you can't control everything.

I shrugged and flipped the switch beside me. The Grand Salon's row of crystal chandeliers blazed into glory.

Angela stomped behind the buffet, still grumbling. "We might as well sing a few bars of 'Stowaway, Here We Come.'"

Then she screamed.

She screamed because she'd been so busy balling out Vannie and Shackleford for being noisy that she'd stepped on the foot of the guy hiding behind the buffet.

Instantly, he sprang over the counter and rushed out my door, knocking me down in the process.

I tried to trip him on my way down but missed. At least I remembered to blow my whistle.

I got halfway up, but Angela and Shackleford came racing after him and knocked me down again.

By the time I caught up to them, Team Two, having heard my whistle, rounded the bow, and Plan 432B worked like a steel trap.

Chesterton raced in front of the guy, causing him to brake just as Shackleford crashed into him from behind. He fell backward and in the confusion, Angela, Vannie and I pinned his arms behind him while Supergranny tied his hands with the extra-strength grosgrain ribbon she carries everywhere.

He was burly, 60ish and extremely cross.

He had thick, black, funny-looking hair, and even without his helmet I recognized him as the rude guy with the cream and orange bike. I just couldn't tell if he was the first rude guy or the second.

"OK, young man," Supergranny said to him, "you're going straight to the Captain."

"Wait a minute," Vannie broke in. "Listen. Something's wrong."

We listened. I didn't hear anything but the river knocking against the hull and the burly guy breathing hard and snorting. Bouncing on the deck when he fell had knocked the wind out of him, and he was still trying to catch up.

"I don't hear anything," Angela said.

"But that's it," Vannie said. "The calliope was halfway through 'Alley Cat,' and it stopped cold."

We all listened again.

Nothing.

Something was definitely wrong. Say what you want about Mazie Mayberry, she never stopped playing calliope in midsong. Never.

Just then an eerie sound broke the stillness. It was Clyde the Crazy Calliope. It sounded as if it were screeching, "Helpppppp."

Up we went to Crazy Clyde the Calliope's platform, a few steps above the top deck.

Supergranny and Chesterton led, followed by the stowaway still guarded by Shackleford, then Vannie, Angela and me.

We got to the top and stopped.

It was not a pretty sight.

Mazie sat at Clyde's bench, staring straight out into the fog. Clarence stood beside her with his hands in the air. Beside them stood the other rude biker, scowling.

He looked exactly like our rude biker, except that instead of having funny-looking black hair, he was as bald as a cantaloupe.

There were two other unfortunate differences:

First, he was wearing Clarence's whistle around his neck.

26

Worse, he was holding a gun. It was pointed straight at Crazy Clyde the Calliope's steam pipes.

"One move from any of you and the calliope gets it," he said in a gruff and nasty voice. "Ping, ping, ping — that calliope will have more holes than a tennis racket."

Nobody moved. Mazie kept staring into the fog, still as a frozen person. I guess she was afraid to blink for fear Clyde would get it in the pipes.

"He took my whistle," Clarence rasped, his hands still in the air.

"Never mind, Clarence," Supergranny said.

"Here now, young man," she said to the bald crook. "Let's be reasonable. That calliope is irreplaceable. A bit of Americana. An antique."

"You bet, sister," he said. "Now untie Romy's hands."

Obviously, as Angela would say, Romy was our stow-away — the one with hair.

Supergranny ignored the order to untie Romy and took another stab at reasoning with Old Baldy. "That calliope is a national treasure," she said. "Louis Armstrong heard it when he went north from New Orleans by riverboat in 1922. Young Bix Beiderbecke used to come down to the river in Davenport, Iowa, to hear it. President Teddy Roosevelt —"

"Can it, sister," Old Baldy cut in. He stopped scowling and changed the look on his face to something like a smile. It was worse than the scowl.

"Of course, we don't want to harm this historic calliope," he cooed in a yucky, sugary voice. "Just do what we ask, and everything will be juuuuust fine."

Then he flipped the safety on the revolver.

27

"Better untie Romy, Joshua," Supergranny said quietly.

I would rather have kicked him in the shin and spit in his eyes, but even I knew that was big-time stupid.

I untied his hands.

The first thing he did was try to kick Shackleford. He was still mad at her for tripping him, I guess. Luckily, Shackleford was too fast for him and got away.

"Now, Romy, you take everybody down to the pilot house," ordered Old Baldy.

"Right, Remy," said Old Hairy.

"Round up the Captain and Second Mate and tell them we're taking over this tub," ordered Old Baldy.

"Right, Remy," said Old Hairy.

"I'll be watching from here. One false move from anybody and Crazy Clyde the Calliope will have more holes than a spaghetti colander. Got it?" barked Old Baldy.

"Right, Remy," said Old Hairy.

Things went downhill from there.

Here I'd thought the morning had been bad because of Supergranny's flu and the slate. That should teach me to know when I'm well-off. Compared to what happened next, the early morning in Supergranny's kitchen had been lunch at Disneyland.

The second worst thing during the next five minutes was the look on Captain Tubweathers' face when the crooks forced us overboard into the skiff. She stared up at that old sourpuss, Romy, with a look I've never seen before and hope I never see again.

But the grand prize worst thing was what happened to Shackleford.

The diabolical duo ordered us all to climb down a ladder

to the skiff. But since Shackleford and Chesterton aren't too swift when it comes to climbing down ladders, Clarence was getting ready to lower them in a basket.

Second Mate and Angela were already in the skiff, waiting to catch them, and I was halfway down the ladder.

Just then Old Hairy Romy finally got a clear shot at Shackleford and took another kick at her. This time Shackleford couldn't get out of the way in time. She yelped and took off around the deck. The next thing we knew, there was a loud splash on the other side.

"DOG OVERBOARD!" Supergranny yelled.

The splash shocked Captain into action.

"Quick, start the motor," she yelled at Second Mate. "We've got to get to the other side to find Shackleford."

Supergranny and Vannie scrambled down into the skiff as I grabbed Chesterton from the basket.

"For Pete's sake, hurry!" Captain yelled at Clarence, who was slowly working his way down the ladder. Finally he made it.

Second Mate ripped the outboard motor cord and the crowded skiff (there were nine of us: Supergranny, Angela, Vannie, Captain, Clarence, Second Mate, Mazie, Chesterton and me) raced to the other side.

The fog was so thick you couldn't see a garage-length in any direction. Second Mate idled the motor and we listened so hard I thought my ears would fall out.

But there wasn't a dog-paddling sound anywhere.

"SHACKLEFORD," Vannie yelled, tears in her eyes. Nothing.

"SHAAAAACKLEFORD," we all yelled, then waited, holding our breath with hope that shaggy old Shackleford would come paddling up through the fog.

Nothing, except the sound of the Riverboat Riverbelle's engines coming to life.

"DON'T-TRY-TO-FOLLOW-US," Old Baldy Remy's voice boomed over a bullhorn. "OR-THIS-CAL-LI-O-PE-WILL-HAVE-MORE-HOLES-THAN-A-CHAIN-LINK-FENCE."

"We'd better head for shore," Supergranny said. "The odds are 99 to 1 Shackleford is already there. Dogs are wonderful swimmers. Besides, we've got to report this to the police."

We chugged slowly to shore, calling for Shackleford as we went. All eyes scanned the water, desperately hoping for a glimpse of that shaggy head.

All eyes, that is, but Captain Tubweathers'. She just stared back at the Riverbelle disappearing into the mist.

6

One thousand impatient bikers waited at the dock.

"Oh, brother," Captain Tubweathers whispered. "How am I going to explain this?"

Remember that some of those bikers had been waiting in line since we loaded the last batch more than an hour before. Remember that we were already 20 minutes late picking up this group. Remember that it was drizzling.

After all that, think how they must have felt when they saw us. Instead of the red and white Riverboat Riverbelle, coming to take them for a river ride, here came a dingy gray skiff. Instead of flying flags and calliope music, here came the most bedraggled eight people plus robot ever to land on the banks of the Mississippi.

As soon as the tangled wall of bikes and bikers caught sight of Captain Tubweathers, a mighty rumble swept through the throng.

It went something like this: "WHAT THE —? Hey, what's going on? Grrrr. Mutter, mutter, mutter. GRRRRR. What the —? Mutter, muttermuttermutter . . ."

Meanwhile, off to the side, one man's voice cut through the mush like a trial lawyer's. "WE DEMAND AN EX-PLANATION," he yelled. "WE DEMAND AN EXPLAN-ATION. WE DEMAND AN EXPLANATION."

Next thing you knew, the crowd had taken up his chant. It was a little ragged at first: "WE DEMAND, Grrr, Mutter-mutter, — planation." Like that. But finally it tightened up, one thousand voices strong.

"WE DEMAND AN EXPLANATION. WE DEMAND AN EXPLANATION. WE DEMAND AN EXPLANA-TION."

The whole thing was getting pretty tense, and I was grateful for the chain holding back the bikers. I understood how they felt, but if they wanted an explanation, they had to shut up. Nobody could be heard above that din.

Someone had to do something. Fast.

"Pyramid!" Supergranny yelled. "Pyramid! Now!"

With that she started organizing a pyramid under the giant "WELCOME TO ROTRATTT" banner stretched above the dock.

"Captain, Clarence, Second Mate and Mazie on bottom," she barked. "Angela and Joshua on their shoulders. Quick!"

She whipped a large red marker out of her purse. "Here, Vannie. Hurry, upsy-daisy to the top."

Before you could say "Demand an explanation," we were in a pyramid with Vannie at the apex, holding the marker. With one foot on my shoulder and the other on Angela's, she could barely reach the white space at the bottom of the WELCOME TO ROTRATTT banner.

"Print 'RIVERBELLE,'" Supergranny shouted. "Big as you can."

Vannie scratched out the letters, big as she could for as far as she could reach. "I can't reach anymore," she gasped. "We have to move down."

"Move four steps," Supergranny shouted.

The pyramid base moved four steps with Angela, Vannie and me hanging on for dear life and Vannie shouting, "WRONG WAY, WRONG WAY."

"DOWNRIVER," Supergranny yelled. "Move downriver."

The base changed course, moved eight steps downriver, and Vannie started writing again.

"Print 'HIJACKED,'" Supergranny yelled.

Vannie printed "Hijacked." At that, ten bikers screamed, a hundred bikers gasped, and a thousand bikers stopped shouting "WE DEMAND AN EXPLANATION."

Our pyramid moved upriver again, and Vannie started another line at Supergranny's direction.

When she was finished the banner read:
WELCOME TO ROTRATTT
RIVERBELLE HIJACKED
ALL BIKERS SAFE
PHONE POLICE

By the time Vannie had written P-O-L-I, one thousand bikers had bolted for the pay telephone by the highway, and Vannie's tennis shoe had carved a permanent cavity in my shoulder.

We dismantled the pyramid and sat down on the dock to wait for the police.

As soon as we sat down, Clarence whipped out the cards.

I couldn't believe it. The Riverbelle had been stolen, Shackleford had fallen overboard and disappeared, and here was Clarence, still busting to play cards.

Supergranny just laughed and told him to deal. "We can't do anything about the Riverbelle or Shackleford until the police get here, anyway," she said. "We might as well play cards."

We got in one quick hand before Officer Inspect, an old friend of Supergranny's, arrived in a squad car. Fortunately, Clarence won. I hoped that would hold him for a while.

*   *   *   *   *   *

It wasn't quite noon yet, and Officer Inspect had already had a very rough day. Later he would call it the day of the biggest crime spree since he joined the force.

"Police headquarters is a madhouse," he said, jumping out of his squad car. "The pig rustlers are back."

"Oh, no," Supergranny said. "Again? How bad is it?"

"Bad," he said. "Very bad. Forty-eight thousand pounds of pig stolen this morning."

"Oh, no," Supergranny said again. "That is bad."

"Yes," he said. "Two hundred and forty 200-pound hogs, valued at $20,880."

Supergranny whistled at the amount.

"On top of that, they got twenty 40-pound feeder pigs," he said.

"Oh, the poor little things," Vannie said.

"Yes. Quite," Officer Inspect said. "But enough about my problems. What's going on down here?"

Supergranny quickly explained about the stolen River-belle with the rest of us filling in the details.

"Twin crooks," Vannie said. "About 60. Identical."

"Except one was bald and one had hair," I said.

"Disguised as bikers," Angela said.

"And they threatened to destroy Clyde," Mazie said.

"Clyde?" Officer Inspect asked.

"The famous Clyde the Crazy Calliope," said Mazie, amazed at his ignorance.

"Oh, yes. Quite," Officer Inspect said.

"And we're very worried about Shackleford," Super-granny said. "Because one of the crooks kicked her and she jumped overboard."

"And they stole my Riverbelle," Captain said softly. "My Riverbelle."

After that, there really wasn't anything else to say.

Officer Inspect put his notepad away and patted the Cap-tain's shoulder.

"Don't worry, Captain Tubweathers, they won't get away with it. They can't hide in this fog forever. And if they go up- or downriver, they'll have to pass through a lock. We'll get them at a lock whichever way they go."

"He's absolutely right, Captain," Supergranny said. "Now you let Mazie and Second Mate take you home for a nice cup of tea. I need Clarence to come with me, and I'll call you from my office in an hour. I have a plan."

With that, Captain, Mazie and Second Mate left for Captain's penthouse apartment above the Riverview Bakery, a few steps away from the dock.

Meanwhile, the rest of us trudged up the hill to the Ferrari. We hadn't taken ten steps when Chesterton went berserk, whirring and chirping and flashing. He jumped out of Angela's tote and raced toward the Ferrari with the rest of us after him.

No wonder he was so excited.

There, stretched out on the Ferrari hood was the wettest, dirtiest, most tangled up Old English sheepdog the world has ever seen.

Good old Shackleford had managed to swim back to the riverbank and find the Ferrari.

Hearing Chesterton's racket, she raised her head, looked toward us, then collapsed on the hood again, too exhausted to move.

"SHACKLEFORD," we screamed, racing up the hill. "SHACKLEFORD! SHACKLEFORD! SHACKLEFORD!!!"

7

The next hour was about the busiest we ever spent in Supergranny's workshop-office-laboratory-playroom-garage.

First, we had to help Clarence hitch the ski boat up to the Ferrari. Then we had to show him how to shift the Ferrari's gears. Then we had to watch as he drove off to the dock.

He'd never driven a Ferrari before, much less a Ferrari pulling a ski boat, and he almost took the mailbox with him as he turned slowly onto the highway from Supergranny's driveway.

I thought Supergranny was going to faint when she saw it, but she didn't. She just groaned.

"Oh, well, let's try not to think about it," she said, meaning try not to think about Clarence loose on the road in her beloved Ferrari.

As soon as Clarence left, I checked in with Mom from the yellow phone booth in Supergranny's office.

"Tell your mother we might be quite late tonight," Supergranny said. "We probably won't make it back for dinner."

Mom said that was OK as long as we stayed with Mrs. Oglepop and were home by bedtime.

I hung up and went over to the washtub to help Angela and Vannie groom Shackleford. They'd just pulled her out of the bathwater and were preparing to attack her mats, armed with a fleet of dog combs and brushes and three hair dryers.

"Take this," Angela said grimly, handing me a hair dryer and assigning me a third of Shackleford to work on.

I'd seen Shackleford matted before, but this was ridiculous.

She looked worse than a blackberry bush at a knot-tying tournament. On top of that, she was tired and grumpy from her terrifying morning, and she fussed at every little pull of the comb.

We did the best we could in the time we had. Some of the mats we had to let go, and some we had to cut out.

Chesterton ran between us with the scissors, whirring and chirping at Shackleford to stand still, whirring and chirping at us to hurry and, in general, getting on everyone's nerves.

Meanwhile, Supergranny sat at her desk, poring over the latest copy of "Upper Mississippi River Navigation Charts."

"Hmmmm," she'd mutter now and then, "Blue Heron

Island . . ." Or, "Hmmmm . . . Goose Pond." Or, "Hmmmm . . . wing dam."

Shackleford was still damp when she jumped up and called us over to the desk.

"OK, here's Plan 327A," she said. "We start with aerial reconnaissance."

"Oreo what?" I asked.

"Recon who?" Vannie asked.

"I beg your pardon?" Angela asked.

"Aerial reconnaissance," she repeated. "That means we'll fly up and down the river between the two locks and see whether we can spot the Riverbelle.

"Now, your jobs. Please pay strict attention, because we only have time to go through this once.

"Angela, call the Coast Guard on Line 2 to see if the river fog has lifted. There's no sense going up if the fog is too dense to see anything."

"Right," Angela said.

"Joshua, study these charts so you'll be able to spot islands and so forth from the air."

"Right," I said.

"Vannie, get us some raisins from the 'Healthy Snack' vending machine. We've missed lunch and need something to tide us over."

"Right," Vannie said.

"Chesterton, go push the 'Helicopter Pad' button in the southeast corner."

Chesterton chirped.

"Shackleford, you look terrible. Shake yourself or something."

Shackleford shook.

39

Supergranny looked at her watch. "While you're doing that, I'll phone Captain and Officer Inspect on Line 1. Let's all meet at the southeast corner in five minutes."

I sat down at the desk with the river charts while the others took off in six thousand directions.

The charts showed every island, lock and dam on the river and had a red line down the middle, showing the main channel where the towboats and barges go. It also showed where all the rivers and creeks flowed into the Mississippi and even had street maps of the towns along the shore.

While I studied the maps, Shackleford shook and re-shook, and Vannie climbed up to the Vending Machine Balcony for our raisins. The balcony has tier upon tier of hot and cold vending machines: "Healthy Snacks," "Junk Food Snacks," "Ice Cream Math," and on and on, too many to mention. You can get anything from pizza to prime rib to Shrimp Hong Sue, Angela's favorite disgusting Chinese dish.

By then, breakfast seemed several weeks past, and I was hungry enough to eat three pizzas or even a platter of Shrimp Hong Sue, but there wasn't time if we were going to save the Riverbelle and Clyde.

Before I knew it, it was time to meet the others in the southeast corner.

Some people think the southeast corner is the best part of Supergranny's office. It's separated from the rest of the room by a white picket fence.

The fence has a long list of activities painted on it with a button beside each one. There are dozens and dozens of them, such as Roller Rink, Basketball Court, Swimming Pool, Helicopter Pad . . . you get the idea.

Operating instructions are posted on the fence:

1. Lock the gate.
2. Push the button beside the activity you want.

Of course, Chesterton had already taken care of that. He had pushed the button beside "Helicopter Pad." Instantly, a yellow and white curtain had fallen. Before you could say "Upper Mississippi River Navigation Chart" it had risen again, and there, on the other side of the fence, was Supergranny's gleaming helicopter with its red, white and blue propeller.

We unlocked the gate and climbed aboard. Supergranny took the controls.

"Angela, do the honors," Supergranny said, pointing at a star-shaped flashing button on the helicopter control panel.

Angela pushed the button and the southeast corner ceiling retracted to reveal bright blue sky.

"The Coast Guard said the sky is clear at the river, too," Angela said. "A wonderful day for helicoptering."

"Great," Supergranny shouted above the whir of the propeller. "The fog is gone, and the sun is out. Look out, Old Baldy and Hairy. Things are starting to go our way."

With that, we lifted smoothly into the sky, dipped slightly toward our house next door, then headed straight for the river.

8

The fog had lifted, the sun had come out — and the Riverbelle had disappeared.

"It's *got* to be down there somewhere," Supergranny said for the tenth time, turning the helicopter around above Lock and Dam 15. "Officer Inspect said only two large barges have locked through today — the Homer T. Dusenberry and S. L. Twain. So the Riverbelle *has* to be here . . . somewhere."

She meant that the Riverbelle was trapped between two locks. The locks and dams were built across the river to even out the depth enough for barge traffic. But they also worked like fences. There was no way for the Riverbelle to go upriver without passing through Lock 15. And no way to go downriver without passing through Lock 16.

At least, there was no way *we* could think of. Were we missing something?

"Could the crooks have *disguised* the Riverbelle to look like the Homer T. Whatever?" asked Vannie, forgetting the barge tow's last name.

"Possibly," Supergranny answered, "except the lockmaster knows both tows and their crews. He's positive they were the real Homer T. Dusenberry and S. L. Twain."

"I hate to ask this, Supergranny," Angela said, "but could the Riverbelle have sunk?"

Supergranny shuddered.

"Possibly," she answered, "but we would be able to see it. The river is only about 20 feet at its deepest, and the Riverbelle is taller than that. Even if she sat right down on the bottom, we'd be able to see her smokestack and part of her upper deck."

She straightened the helicopter, and we started downriver again.

"Let's go through Plan 327A again," she said. "Maybe we missed something last time."

Plan 327A worked like this: Supergranny flew the helicopter, and Vannie, Angela and I took turns reading the navigation chart aloud while the other two checked the river through binoculars. Meanwhile, Shackleford and Chesterton sat back and enjoyed the ride.

For all the good Plan 327A was doing, the rest of us might as well have sat back and enjoyed the ride, too. We had already been over every inch of the river and hadn't seen a trace of the Riverbelle. Where do you hide a riverboat as big as an apartment building? We were completely baffled.

"OK, Joshua," Supergranny said. "Let's get started."

It was my turn to read the charts. I turned back to page 88 just as we flew over the bridge. A few straggling ROTRATTT bikers were still crossing it on their way back to the baseball stadium.

"Pelican Island to starboard," I read from the chart.

"Check," said Vannie, peering through her binoculars. "Nothing unusual. Just some people fishing."

"Credit Island to starboard," I read.

"Check," Angela said. "Just some people golfing."

One of the surprising things about seeing the Mississippi from the air is how many islands and marshy inlets and ponds it has. Places with names like Enchanted Island, Goose Pond . . . and on and on. And some of them are huge, like Credit Island, for instance, which is big enough to hold a golf course with plenty of picnic space left over.

By now we were already on the outskirts of town. The houses thinned out to a few scattered farmhouses on one side of the river and a rugged state forest on the other.

There was a break in the trees for the Little Cove Marina. Dozens of boats bobbed gently at their moorings. We flew over them slowly. There were some good-sized houseboats and one *very* expensive seagoing yacht, but nothing half as big as the Riverbelle.

We circled the marina twice to be sure, then started back downriver.

The old Mississippi sparkled in the afternoon sun. It was in a changed mood entirely from the misty, mushy mess it had been that morning.

A dozen or so sailboats tacked smoothly in the breeze, and the shadow of our helicopter slid across their sails. In the distance we spotted the Homer T. Dusenberry barge, 100 feet long and loaded down with golden grain, bound for New Orleans.

Now we were over a stretch of river far from town.

"Andalusia Island, Goose Pond to port," I read.

"Nothing, except — quick, look — a blue heron," Angela shouted. I put down the chart long enough to watch the heron glide along the marshy Andalusia Slough, then disappear into the dark green trees.

On we went.

"Velie Chute," I read.

"Nothing," chorused Angela and Vannie.

"Magic Island," I read.

"Nothing but the green smokestack," Vannie said.

"And an empty duck blind offshore," Angela added.

"WHAT?" Supergranny asked suddenly. "Repeat that!"

"Velie Chute to port?" I asked.

"No, no, after that," Supergranny said.

"An empty duck blind off Magic Island?" Angela asked.

"No, no, before that," Supergranny said. "Vannie, you said something."

Vannie looked blank. "I can't remember. All I said was there's nothing on Magic Island but the smokestack."

"SMOKESTACK! THAT'S IT! SMOKESTACK!" Supergranny shouted.

"But it's just the same green smokestack we've seen every time we've flown over today," Vannie said.

"I know, I know, but it didn't click before," Supergranny said. "There's no bridge to Magic Island, no roads anywhere *near* Magic Island. So why would there be a smokestack on such a desolate part of the river?"

"A fishing cabin, maybe?" I asked.

"A fishing cabin would have a chimney, maybe a flue — but Vannie said 'smokestack.' Why would a fishing cabin have anything as tall as a smokestack?"

By then she'd turned the helicopter around and was headed back to Magic Island for a better look.

Down, down we went, so low I felt I could stick out my foot and kick the treetops. I just hoped she knew how to spot smokestacks and fly helicopters at the same time. I also hoped we'd spot it the first time over, because I'm not crazy about flying that close to trees.

We almost missed it. It was the same color as the dark green treetops, and you could barely see it poking above them.

"Strange," Supergranny said excitedly. "Extremely, extraordinarily, totally strange."

"One more look," she said, turning the helicopter and heading back again, lower than ever.

"JOSHUA HAS HIS EYES SHUT; JOSHUA HAS HIS EYES SHUT," yelled Mega-Mouth Vannie.

My eyes flew open just in time for our best view yet of the smokestack. It had curlicues around the rim and looked freshly painted. But we couldn't see what it was the smokestack *of* because the trees were so dense and were laced together with leafy wild grapevines.

Vannie-The-Mouth missed it entirely because she'd been so busy harassing me about my eyes being shut she forgot to look, which served her right, in my opinion.

"All those curlicues around the rim; they were as fancy as the Riverbelle's smokestack," Angela said excitedly.

"They could have painted the smokestack green before we got here," I said.

"They could have sailed into a Magic Island inlet under cover of fog," Supergranny said. "Quick, Joshua, is there an inlet on the charts?"

I took a closer look at Magic Island. "Pirate's Pond," I said triumphantly. "It's bigger than Goose Pond on Andalusia Island and it opens near the main river channel. It *might* be wide and deep enough for the Riverbelle."

"Then they *could* have sailed into Magic Island during the fog and painted the smokestack green to hide it," Vannie yelled excitedly.

"It's the best lead we have," Supergranny said. "It's time for a closer look."

I groaned. "How much closer can we get? We almost sat in the trees last time."

Supergranny laughed. "Not by air, by boat," she said. She opened the helicopter full throttle and before you could say Homer T. Dusenberry twenty times we were landing on the dock near the spot where Clarence had parked the Ferrari and speedboat. He was sitting in the boat, playing solitaire on a tackle box.

"Clarence, would you please help the kids get the boat in the water?" Supergranny asked. "We have a sudden urge to water-ski down by Magic Island."

9

But Captain Tubweathers wouldn't let us leave.

"No you don't. Not yet," she told Supergranny.

She'd been watching for us from her penthouse above the bakery. As soon as she saw the helicopter, she zipped down to the dock in the Babybelle.

Babybelle (named after the Riverbelle, of course) is her red and white golf cart. Because of her knee injury, Captain can't walk very fast. So when she's in a real hurry, she whips around on Babybelle.

"Now don't argue, Sadie," she said to Supergranny. "You're not taking these children out on that river until you all have a decent meal."

"But, Captain —" Supergranny said.

"No buts to it," Captain insisted. "I know you're trying to save the Riverbelle, and I'm grateful. But you've already missed lunch. If you're going to confront those twin thugs, you need a good supper to keep up your strength."

"But, Captain —" Supergranny said.

"Just one-half hour," Captain said. "Thirty minutes. That's all I ask. You just have to sit down, eat, get up and leave. I've already taken the chicken out of the oven. Mazie is mashing the potatoes now, and Second Mate has fixed a dozen of his special, double-hot stuffed cabbage rolls.

It sounded great up to the cabbage rolls.

Remember, we hadn't had anything for lunch but a bunch of raisins. I was starving, and who knew how long we'd be out on the river without food? But Second Mate's cabbage rolls! I'd had them once!! Yech!!! And you couldn't just say, "No, thank you very much," or, "No thanks, I'm full," or, "I'm allergic to cabbage."

Oh, no. He wouldn't settle for that. He was so proud of them you *had* to eat one and *rave* about how good it was, or he'd cry and rant and threaten to mutiny and all that.

We were in for it, though, because Supergranny had surrendered, agreed we had to eat sometime, anyway, and was climbing into the cart.

"You're right. What's half an hour more or less?" she said to Captain.

Angela, Vannie and I climbed on after her, and the Babybelle bumped along the sand with Chesterton, Shackleford and Clarence trotting along beside.

"Not me," Clarence kept muttering to himself. "I'll never eat another one of those cabbage rolls. Never."

It turned out to be a great meal in spite of the cabbage rolls.

We ate at the long table on Captain's balcony, over-looking the river. Mazie had set it with flowers and candles in net-covered bottles. It was loaded down with baked chicken, mashed potatoes, green beans, lime Jell-O, hot biscuits, chocolate cake . . . and cabbage rolls.

Captain and Mazie had even set up a low table in the corner for Shackleford and Chesterton. It was loaded with platters of dog chow, milk bones, gum drops . . . and cabbage rolls.

"Now dive in," Captain ordered, giving Supergranny, Angela, Vannie and me the bench on the side of the table facing the river. She, Mazie, Clarence and Second Mate sat down opposite us.

While we ate, Supergranny filled them in about the mysterious smokestack on Magic Island.

"It's a slim lead, but it's all we have so far," she said.

Then Captain filled us in on Officer Inspect's latest report.

"There's still no sign of the Riverbelle at either lock," she said. "But they fed our description of the twins into the National Crime Center computer. The computer suspects the Twittles."

"The Whattles?" Clarence asked.

"The Twittle Twins, Romy and Remy, nicknamed after Romulus and Remus, legendary twin founders of Rome," Captain answered. "Notorious pair of thugs with arrest records as long as a barge pole. But no convictions."

"No convictions?" Supergranny asked.

"None," Captain answered. "They always get off. Time and again the police will have forty pounds of evidence against them. Time and again, they come up with a fifty-pound alibi.

"For instance, last June they were arrested for robbing a California bank. Thirteen eyewitnesses. And what happened? At the exact time of the robbery one of them had fainted in a crowded movie lobby. Ninety-seven witnesses, counting three ushers and the ambulance driver, swore Twittle One was at the movies at the time of the robbery."

"Strange," Supergranny said.

"It was the same story the year before in Nevada," Captain went on. "Remember the Kitty Kat Casino nickel slot machine heist? Three show girls and an ex-governor thought they saw the Twittles dragging heavy canvas sacks out of the casino, spilling a trail of nickels behind them. But it turned out Twittle Two was having a tooth pulled in Hurricane, Utah, at the time. The dentist swore to it."

"Odd," Supergranny said.

"Not to change the subject, but what about the pigs?" Vannie asked. "The ones that were rustled."

"Oh, yes, the pignapping," Captain said. "Bad news there, too. The police and sheriff's department are stumped. By the way, they belonged to Riverdale farm. You remember Roscoe Riverdale, Sadie. I think you went to school with him."

"Of course, poor Roscoe," Supergranny said, her fork toying with a cabbage roll. "He always loved pigs."

"And still does, poor soul," Captain said. "He farms Riverdale with his children and grandchildren. They *all* love pigs. They're probably the best hog producers in the county. It's a terrible blow to them.

"Anyway, the police can't find a trace of Roscoe's hogs," Captain went on. "They vanished like my Riverbelle, poof — gone with the fog."

51

"Haven't the police found tracks or anything?" Angela asked.

"Well, yes. That's the strange part about it. They did. Hog tracks, in fact. Leading from the hog confinement building down to the river."

"The river?" Supergranny asked.

"Yes, strange isn't it? Two crimes. Same day. Both involve the river."

"The river and fog . . . ," Supergranny said.

While they were talking I was watching Shackleford and Chesterton in the corner at their low table. They'd polished off the gumdrops, milk bones and dog chow, and Shackleford was sniffing the cabbage rolls.

Chesterton had turned his whirring and beeping volume down to "whisper" and was whirring and beeping away at Shackleford. I couldn't tell if he was egging him on to eat the cabbage rolls or warning him not to. But the next thing I knew, there was a faint splash and their trays were clean. I'd have bet forty dollars that two cabbage rolls were polluting the river.

Supergranny, who had managed to down her cabbage roll, took a look at our plates and tried to save us.

"Well, I hate to eat and run," she said, hopping up. "But we've got to get moving."

Mazie, knowing how we hated cabbage rolls and being a kind woman, tried to help by bustling around, clearing the table.

But Second Mate was too shrewd for them.

"STOP!" he bellowed. "The kids haven't finished their cabbage rolls."

He stood at the end of the table, folded his arms and waited. The balcony became terribly still. Shackleford and Chesterton watched smugly from their corner.

It was either eat the darned things, sit there all night or have Second Mate collapse in hysterics.

Angela ate her cabbage roll.

Vannie ate her cabbage roll.

I ate my cabbage roll.

Second Mate still stood there, arms folded, waiting.

Eating his cabbage rolls was not enough, not by miles. You had to brag about them, too.

But what could you say about something that tasted like burnt shoes wrapped in spicy clarinet reeds? I mean, what could you say without telling a genuine, world cup, triple-whopper lie?

Angela went first, her voice tiptoeing on the ledge between hurting a friend and telling a lie.

"Second Mate," she said, "I do believe those cabbage rolls were as good as the last ones you made."

Next came Vannie, her eyes still watering from the cabbage rolls' double picante hot sauce.

"Second Mate," she said. "Nobody makes cabbage rolls like you do."

Drat. Why couldn't I have thought of that? Now it was my turn. There he stood. Arms folded. Waiting.

I gulped more iced water.

"Unforgettable," I gasped. "Your cabbage rolls are unforgettable."

It was the best I could do, and, luckily, it worked. He smiled. He grinned. He hugged us goodbye, clicked his heels and insisted on doing the dishes. He was the world's happiest cabbage-roll maker.

"Thanks for being so kind to Second Mate," Captain whispered as we headed down the stairs. "Don't worry. I've got a bottle of Pepto-Bismol stashed in the Babybelle."

10

We roared away from the dock with Captain and Clarence waving us off from the Babybelle.

Shackleford and Chesterton sat in the bow, wearing yellow life jackets like the rest of us.

Shackleford's dunking that morning had not dampened her love of boating one millimeter. Her round, black, buttony nose pointed firmly ahead, she sat like a statue, too happy to move as the wind whipped through her hair.

Chesterton, on the other hand, was too happy to sit still. He hopped and fidgeted and begged Supergranny to cross-cut the other boats' waves to make our ski boat jump.

"Just once more, Chesterton," Supergranny said with a laugh, aiming the ski boat diagonally at the wake of a large cruiser.

Theerudd, Theerudd, THEERUDD, we skimmed the wake, with Chesterton hopping and whirring and the rest of us laughing, hanging on and holding our breath.

"Enough horsing around," Supergranny shouted at Chesterton. She headed the boat downriver. "We've got pirates to catch!

"Of course, there's no law against enjoying the ride in the meantime," she added. "Look at this! Just look!"

She meant look at the river. Supergranny is almost as goofy over the river as the Captain. And she likes other people to go goofy over it, too. I mean, she delights in getting her clutches on visitors who have never seen the Mississippi before. She always wants to be the first to take them on a boat ride, or across the bridge or for a walk along the bank.

Then she's like Second Mate with his cabbage rolls. She expects them to brag. And I don't mean just say, 'How lovely,' and go on talking about stock prices or Central America. I mean brag and brag hard. About all the shades of pink in a river sunset. Or about the silver glint of the water. Or about how funny the wild ducks are, crowding up to the rocks in the evening.

You just can't over-brag the river as far as Supergranny is concerned. Lay it on as thick as you want, then double it. To her, the old Mississippi deserves every word.

And I've got to admit, that evening the river was really showing off. The sky was already turning thirty-seven shades of pink. But unfortunately, none of us were going to be lucky enough to think much about the sunset. Especially me. In fact, it turned out to be the most unpleasant sunset I've ever lived through.

We stopped enjoying the sunset and started getting down to business just before the bend in the river above Magic Island.

Supergranny cut the engine, I scrunched down on my stomach in the bottom of the boat, and Angela jumped overboard.

It was the start of Plan 491A.

"Remember, we're supposed to look like your typical, everyday water-skiers," Supergranny whispered.

"Right," Angela said, bobbing around in the water.

"Right," I said, trying to get used to peering through Supergranny's powerful, portable periscope. The periscope is like the kind on submarines except it's much smaller. Also, instead of looking through it from underwater as they do in submarines, I was using it to look over the side of the boat.

The idea was that *if* the pirate pair were on Magic Island, and *if* they were watching us with binoculars, it would be ten thousand times better if they didn't see us watching them back.

I mean, it would arouse their suspicion. Put them on guard. All that.

So I used the periscope. From a distance, its chrome head should blend with the chrome cleats and knobs on the boat. We hoped.

Supergranny whispered instructions to Angela one last time.

"Remember, we circle in midriver, then pass between the duck blind and Magic Island. First time around, just ski normally. Second time, when we get near Magic Island, pretend to have trouble and fall. That will give us an excuse to stop for a closer look. Got it?"

"Got it," Angela said from the water.

"Good luck," Supergranny said. She stepped over me, sat down in the driver's seat, and turned the motor to idle. "Tell me when she gets the skis on and signals thumbs up," she said to Vannie.

We waited about a minute. The bottom of the boat already felt like it was pressing permanent tracks in my stomach, and we hadn't even started yet. I peered at the trees through the periscope and tried not to think about it.

"Thumbs up," Vannie yelled. We were off!

After a couple of wide circles in midchannel, we headed for the chute, a narrow waterway between the duck blind and Magic Island. First time around, I couldn't see anything but a bunch of leaves and tree bark whipping by. By the second time around, all the trees whizzing past the periscope were starting to make me queasy. My stomach was almost ready to remember the cabbage rolls when Angela faked her fall and we stopped to pick her up.

Supergranny, Vannie, Shackleford and Chesterton made a great noisy fuss about fishing Angela and the skis out of the water. Meanwhile, I lay in the bottom of the boat, trying to blend with the floats and oars while I whipped the periscope head around, searching like mad for some sign of the Riverbelle.

Angela dragged out climbing into the boat as long as possible to give me more time. Finally, she got herself all the way in, and we chugged upriver around the bend, where Supergranny debriefed us.

"Well?" she asked.

"I didn't see the Riverbelle," I said. "But I'm sure I saw something moving behind the trees. I think it was watching us, but I couldn't tell what it was. Maybe it was only a deer or even a bird, but it moved."

"Angela?" Supergranny asked.

"I couldn't see anything," Angela said, drying herself with a towel. "But I think I smelled something."

"Me, too," Vannie said. "In fact I'm sure I smelled something. It smelled like a farm."

Angela agreed excitedly. "Yes, it smelled like . . . live-stock."

"Pigs," Vannie yelled, forgetting to keep her voice down. "It smelled like a lot of pigs!"

11

MAGIC ISLAND

"One of us has to get onto that island," Supergranny said grimly.

She looked slowly around the boat.

Uh-oh. I knew what was coming. I could feel it, as sure as I could feel cold little shivers scampering up my spine.

"If the crooks *are* on Magic Island, they surely have spotted our boat by now . . . ," Supergranny said slowly.

"And they surely have seen Supergranny, Vannie and me," Angela said, thinking aloud.

"And they surely have seen Shackleford because he's too big and hairy to miss. . . ," Vannie put in.

"And they surely have seen Chesterton because he's so hyper and noisy . . . ," Supergranny added.

Her voice trailed off. They all stared at me.

"Any volunteers?" Supergranny chirped.

Oh, brother — volunteers! There I was, the only one left, the only one who had been hiding in the bottom of the boat, the only one the crooks couldn't have seen — and she asked for volunteers.

They wanted me to "volunteer" to singlehandedly land on a dark, forested, crook-infested island. By myself. In my bathing trunks.

For two cents I would have sat there in the bottom of the boat with my mouth shut. Then I thought of the look on the Captain's face when the Riverbelle disappeared in the mist that morning.

I thought of that 60-year-old twin jerk kicking Shackleford.

I thought of how cramped and bored I was sitting in the bottom of the boat with them all staring at me.

I thought, "What the heck."

OK," I said. "Let's go."

Next thing I knew, we were racing around the bend again with me still scrunched down in the bottom of the boat, and Angela skiing along behind.

This time I wore flippers, goggles and a waterproof pack belted over my bathing trunks. It contained a change of clothes, a flashlight, a pack of raisins and a few other crucial things.

We made one wide circle in midriver. When we got near the duck blind, Angela fell as planned, and we went back to pick her up. We were still on the river side of the duck blind.

The idea was that the blind would block the view of anyone watching from the island. We hoped.

Angela paddled over to the island side of the boat, and Supergranny made a big show of helping her aboard.

"NOW!" Supergranny hissed without looking at me.

Why, oh why, had I ever left Cleveland?

But it was too late to complain about that now. I held my nose, rolled over the far side of the boat and splashed into the bone-chilling Mississippi. I surfaced, gulped a lungful of air, then swam underwater for the duck blind about ten feet away.

Supergranny and the others kept making a big hullabaloo about getting Angela into the boat until I was safely inside the duck blind.

As soon as I got inside, I gave them a thumbs up, and Supergranny winked. Angela, who had been pretending to be stuck with one leg aboard and the other in the water, quickly clamored into the boat. Supergranny started the motor and with another quick wink toward the duck blind, they were off. Vannie gave me a quick "thumbs up" behind her back as they roared away.

The duck blind was about the size of a giant doghouse. It was a wood frame laced with tree branches. Hunters had made it to hide in during duck hunting season. They probably sat for hours in the thing every October, peering out the holes between the branches, waiting for some unsuspecting mallard to fly over on its way to breakfast.

The hunters had one major fringe benefit that I didn't have. They sat in a boat. The duck blind was built so they could move a small boat right inside and sit snug as groundhogs.

I would have given a lot to be sitting in a boat right then.

I would have given a lot more to be sitting almost any-place else, but if it had to be here, I would rather have been sitting in a boat. I pulled myself partway up the frame to rest my legs and dry out a little.

It was not the world's most comfortable position. All I could do was hang on. And wait.

It had gotten very quiet in this part of the river.

I could hear some faint noise down near the south end of the island where Supergranny and the others were set-ting up a diversion.

The idea was for them to draw the crooks' attention and in the confusion, I would make a secret landing.

After what seemed about a year and a half, but was prob-ably only about five minutes, I heard the signal — three sharp barks from Shackleford.

Then silence.

Then three more sharp barks, followed by lots of yell-ing and whooping. Shackleford's barking was the signal for me to swim to the island.

The yelling and whooping sounded faint up here, but, I hoped, was spectacular and attention-getting at the ac-tual scene of the whooping.

I pushed myself to the island side of the duck blind and scanned the rocky beach about thirty feet away. It looked deserted as a tomb.

I let go of the blind and swam silently toward Magic Island.

12

MAGIC ISLAND

I arrived.

The swim wasn't bad, and I wasn't even very tired when I got there. Terrified, yes, but not tired. It wasn't far, and the last part was very shallow.

Of course, the current pushed me downstream some, but we had planned for that. I waded onto the rocks at almost the bull's-eye of our landing target.

My orders were:

A. Find a hiding place.

B. Signal.

"*Before* you catch your breath, *before* you change your clothes, *before* you do anything, get yourself out of plain view, then signal us that you're OK," Supergranny had said.

I knew I had to work fast because she had given me only seventeen minutes max after Shackleford's final bark to get to the beach and signal.

If I went one minute over, she'd figure something was wrong, panic, and the whole caboodle of them would swoosh back to the rescue, blasting my cover.

I ducked behind the nearest maple tree and cut a long stick from a thicket of debris. Then I quickly tied Supergranny's red, white, and blue silk Gucci scarf to it like a flag. Her friend Myrtle Witherspoon Richmont* had brought it to her from Rome, and she carried it everywhere. It was part of the crucial equipment in my waterproof pack.

I climbed to the maple's lowest limb, stretched out on my stomach and waved the scarf over the water.

Nothing.

Drat.

I climbed one limb higher and waved the thing again.

Mercifully, this time they saw it. There were three quick barks from Shackleford, silence, then three more quick barks.

Passers-by and pirates would think Shackleford was just doing some general barking, but it was really Ski Boat Control's way of telling me they had received my signal. We'd spent an entire weekend in Supergranny's office teaching Shackleford how to do it in case we ever needed it.

I declimbed the tree and decided I deserved a couple of minutes to rest and shake with terror, which I did.

Then I took off the wet trunks, slathered myself with mosquito repellent, and put on my sweat suit. I hid the

---

*More about Myrtle Witherspoon Richmont in "Supergranny: The Mystery of the Shrunken Heads."

fins and goggles in the underbrush, packed the trunks, scarf and mosquito repellent in the bag, and sat down for a few more minutes of serious shaking.

The sunset was turning from pink to scarlet, and the island was filling up with the murky shadows of dusk. I would be lucky to have another half hour of daylight.

Magic Island, which had looked sleepy and deserted from the river, now seemed alive.

I sat quietly and tried to sort the sounds.

There was the river lapping behind me, sometimes breaking its rhythm with a loud splat against the rocks.

There was a bright red cardinal chattering and singing in a nearby treetop.

From the island interior came a riot of birdcalls, strange and rich, like sounds from a tropical jungle.

And somewhere there was a low, inhuman murmuring. It came and went, and it was a sound I knew but couldn't place. What was it?

Meanwhile, there was the static of twenty million mosquitoes, trying to eat me right through my sweat suit, mosquito repellent and all.

The cardinal moved to my maple tree. "Time-to-go-time-to-go-time-to-go," he seemed to sing.

He was right. It was time to explore the island. Now or never.

I stood.

A squirrel shot out of the leaves in front of me.

"Just a squirrel, just a squirrel, just a squirrel," I told my thudding heart.

The cardinal sang on.

I crossed to the next tree and grabbed it.

The crows and jays and blackbirds still screamed like jungle demons deep in the island.

I started again and made it past three more trees.

Everything went on as before.

I kept going for five trees, then pulled from my pocket the picture of Magic Island I'd torn from the navigation chart. It didn't show much, but at least it gave me a general idea of the shape of the island.

"Time-to-go," chanted the bossy cardinal.

I inched through the underbrush, crawling over rotted logs and squeezing between small trees and bushes, always trying to keep the sound of the river about ten feet to my right.

Gradually, the sound of Supergranny and the rest whooping it up on the ski boat became sharper. I knew I was approaching the south end of the island.

There was a large clearing. I slithered around the edge, then spotted a large rock just beyond it.

My thudding heart stopped.

On the rock with his back to me sat Romy, his tangled black hair glinting purple and blue in the sunset. He sat as still and lumpy as the rock itself, and he held binoculars to his evil little eyes.

He was watching every move of the ski boat's crew through a break in the trees. The diversion had worked, and we had found the pirate's hideout.

Now to find the Riverbelle. And get word to Officer Inspect. And capture Romy and Remy, and their gang if any. And do it without getting caught myself.

"Time-to-go-time-to-go," trilled the cardinal.

"Oh, shut up," I muttered under my breath.

13

I backed quietly into the forest, praying that Romy wouldn't turn around. A twig snapped under my foot. I froze. Hearing something, Romy put down the binoculars and glanced at some squirrels chasing up a tree. Then he went back to peering through the binoculars.

The squirrels saved me. He thought they had made the noise. I retreated quickly under cover of their chatter.

I made my way back to the maple by the shore. I fished Supergranny's spool of black grosgrain ribbon out of the waterproof pack and tied one end of it around the maple. The plan was for me to unroll it as I searched for the Riverbelle. Then it would be my guide back in the darkness.

"The old Tom-Sawyer-and-Becky-Thatcher-cave-trick," Supergranny said. "If it was good enough for them in Mac-Dougal's Cave, it's good enough for us."

Reluctantly I left the comforting sound of the river and began inching my way deep into the dark island, unwinding the ribbon on the ground as I went.

Night was closing in. Bats swooped and dived above me, out for an evening banquet of Magic Island mosquitoes.

Already I was having trouble seeing, but I didn't dare use my flashlight.

I could still hear the faint sounds of Ski Boat Control cavorting in the river, keeping Romy busy. Unfortunately, it was only Romy. Where was Remy, the hairless twin?

A grapevine caught my ankle and I sprawled into a marshy puddle.

Things wiggled under my palms.

Things, things, things shot between my fingers.

In horror, I jumped up and threw my arms around a tree before I even realized what the *things* were. Snakes. Baby snakes. Snakes slithering through my fingers. I'd fallen on a nest of snakes!

I shuddered. I closed my eyes and just stood there.

Little baby garter snakes, and there I was, shuddering and hanging onto a tree.

On the other hand, how did I know they were just garter snakes? Of course, they looked just like the garter snakes we have in the ravine at home. But it was so dark, how could I tell for sure?

Anyway, whatever they were, they would not be poisonous. I'd heard somewhere that Illinois didn't have poisonous snakes. Or I thought I'd heard that somewhere. I hoped I'd heard it somewhere.

Then again, Angela had done a report on rattlesnakes,

and she'd interviewed a man who said he had killed a rattler north of here.

And somewhere I'd read there had been a rattlesnake hunt in Iowa. If true, that probably meant there were rattlesnakes in Iowa, or why would they be hunting them? And Iowa was just on the other side of the river. For all the rattlesnakes knew, Magic Island was *in* Iowa.

Fortunately, these snakes hadn't rattled. Swished a little, but hadn't rattled. Did baby rattlesnakes rattle? Maybe they didn't rattle till, say, adolescence? I wished I knew. I really wished I knew if baby rattlesnakes rattled.

I also wished I didn't think so much. I have a problem with thinking too much. Standing there holding onto that tree, I wished all those snake thoughts would stop racing through my head. I wished I had a switch to turn them off and turn on music or something instead. I wondered if other people had switches like that in their heads and I were the only one who didn't. Maybe there had been a foul-up somehow and my switch had been left out.

Then I wished I'd stop wondering about switches in people's heads.

I knew what I had to do. Whenever thoughts start chasing through my head in circles, I have to take some kind of action: move and do things. That's the only thing that breaks the chain and helps my mind move on to something more sensible.

I started by poking around on the ground with the toe of my tennis shoe for the spool of grosgrain ribbon. I'd dropped it when the grapevine got me.

Finally I nudged it, picked it up, let go of the tree and started out again.

I closed my eyes tight for several seconds, and when I opened them the island didn't seem so dark. I went very slowly, looking all around me and especially at the ground before each step. I didn't want to go sprawling again and land in another nest of you-know-what.

The inhuman murmuring sound was getting louder, and there was a light peeping through the branches ahead. It was so bright, I didn't know how I had missed it before.

The smell we had noticed from the boat was getting worse. Overpowering, in fact. By now, I thought I knew the source, but I had to get closer to be sure.

Suddenly, I came onto a path leading directly toward the light. Probably the path Romy used to go to the south end of the island. It was tempting to use it, but too dangerous.

What if Romy came strolling up behind me?

And I couldn't risk crossing it and leaving my grosgrain ribbon trail there for him to trip over.

I veered away from the path, then worked steadily toward the light. The underbrush was thick and thorny, and the going was rough. It took me a long time to go the last ten feet, but at last I came to the edge of a bank on what had to be Pirate's Pond. I peered through the leaves.

It was a perfect view.

Weird. Sinister. And a perfect view.

14

The pond was lighted like a stage.

Battery-operated floodlights lighted the clearing and cast flickering shadows on the surrounding trees.

Filling the pond and the clearing was the Riverboat Riverbelle — or what had been the Riverboat Riverbelle.

It was hard to believe this was the same proud, regal, bright red and white Riverbelle we had ridden that morning.

For one thing, it was dirty. Really dirty, as in filthy and disgusting. For another, it smelled. For a third, it was stuffed with green-speckled hogs. That's right, green-speckled hogs. Hundreds of green-speckled hogs.

Hogs gobbling grain from buckets. Feeder pigs playing chase on the stairs. Two-ton prizewinning porkers snoozing on top of the pilot house.

Hogs everywhere. Hogs, hogs, hogs, hogs, hogs. And more hogs.

Hogs strolling, grunting, staring, pooping, squealing and making that inhuman murmuring sound I'd heard earlier.

It didn't take a genius to figure out they were the hogs that had been rustled from Roscoe Riverdale's farm under cover of fog that morning.

And I had a pretty good idea how.

They'd been driven right down to the river and herded up the gangplank of the hijacked Riverbelle. Then the Riverbelle had zipped into the pond at Magic Island before the fog lifted.

Slick.

And sleazy.

All day, the captured hogs had been penned up in the poor Riverbelle, and they were wrecking it. I dreaded to think what the Grand Salon looked like by now.

Of course, you couldn't blame the hogs for the mess. It wasn't their fault. For hogs, they were perfectly well-behaved. They were doing exactly what hogs are supposed to do. What else could you expect?

The real Riverbelle wreckers were on a scaffolding slung over the side of the top deck. They were spray-painting the Riverbelle dull green. In fact, they were almost finished. There was just one patch left about the size of a dining room table. As I watched, they finished it, then leaned back against the scaffolding to smoke cigars and admire their work.

They were Remy and Romy in bathing trunks topped with some kind of see-through body suits that looked like they were made from mosquito netting.

Their sunburned bellies rippled and glistened in the floodlight to match their glistening, sunburned bald heads. Watching them puff cigars and grunt and sweat and chuckle about what they had done to the Riverbelle was enough to change your mind about the hogs. Next to the twins, the hogs didn't seem disgusting at all. If there had been an election for least disgusting, the hogs would have won by a landslide.

On top of all the damage they had done to the poor Riverbelle, the twins had been so sloppy spraying paint that they had accidently gotten paint all over the poor hogs. That explained the green speckles.

I don't know what green paint does to hogs, but it probably clogs their pores, at least. Anyway, it can't be good for them.

I leaned out as far as I dared to get a look at Clyde the Crazy Calliope. I dreaded to think what had happened to him in all this.

But as best as I could tell, he had been covered by a blanket to protect him from paint and pigs. I hoped he was completely covered. A green-speckled, hog-damaged Clyde would break Mazie's heart. Not to mention what it would do to Captain.

As I looked around, trying to take it all in, two questions tugged like undertows at the floor of my mind.

First, why two bald heads? Romy had hair — strange black hair.

Second, how had Romy gotten back to the Riverbelle so fast? According to Plan 327B, Supergranny and the others were to keep him busy while I searched for the Riverbelle.

Had he decided they were no threat and left while they were still doing their thing?

But even if he left seconds after I did, how had he gotten back here, changed clothes, climbed up on the scaffolding and started painting so fast? Both crooks were smudged with green paint. They had the look of painters who had been at it a long, long time.

Why?

The first question was easiest. Obviously, (to borrow Angela's word of the week), Romy had worn a wig earlier. It must have been his cockeyed idea of a disguise.

The second question was more troubling: How had the twin on the rock gotten back to the Riverbelle so fast?

Just then, one of the crooks stopped puffing and chuckling and gloating long enough to pull a watch out of his bathing trunks pocket.

"Right on schedule! Get rid of that cigar and get moving. This tub sails for Lock 16 in thirty minutes."

I caught my breath.

Thirty minutes! We had just thirty minutes!

I had to signal Supergranny that I'd found the Riverbelle, she had to notify Officer Inspect, and he had to get here with the Coast Guard to save the Riverbelle.

I took one last look at the poor Riverbelle, then started following my black ribbon trail back into the forest.

I still didn't know everything, but I knew enough: The Riverbelle was here. She'd been painted green. The hogs were here. And they were all heading downriver in thirty minutes.

The island was now totally dark. No moon. No stars. No light. A night like a black pit.

Using my flashlight was tempting, but I was too scared. After all, it was a very small island, and they were very mean crooks.

Running was also tempting. From worry that I wouldn't get the message out in time. From hurry to get it all over with. From . . . fear.

But I forced myself not to run. I forced myself to walk carefully, following the black ribbon.

Back I went through the night toward the beach. Back through the thorns of the berry bushes. Back to the spot near the path, back into the underbrush, back across the marshy lows where the snakes nested, back past the tree where the grapevine tripped me.

At last I heard the welcoming lap of the river against the bank. At last I could see the maple tree on the bank where I'd tied the ribbon. I peered around the tree at the river.

At first I could see nothing but murky darkness. Gradually, one shadow took form against the darkness. They were there. Supergranny and the boat were there.

My heart surged with relief. I fished the flashlight out of the waterproof pack, pointed it at the boat and flicked it on. I passed my hand in front of it, using short and long beams to make Morse Code dots and dashes.

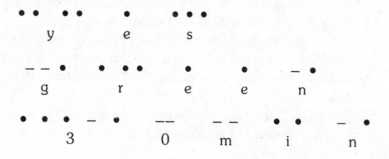

I meant that, yes, the Riverbelle was here, it was painted green and was leaving in 30 minutes. I hoped to high heaven they got it, because I was scared to use the flashlight anymore.

They did. Almost instantly, the signal came back: Three sharp barks from Shackleford, pause, and three more sharp barks.

Passers-by and pirates would think some dog was just doing a little general barking. But it was really Ski Boat Control's way of signaling "message received."

Very quietly, the motor started. Slowly, the shadowy shape of the ski boat moved away, blending into the darkness.

I'd gotten the message out. They were going for help.

Never in my life had I felt so lonely.

I leaned against the tree to wait.

Suddenly, hands shot out of the darkness and grabbed my shoulder. I whirled around. It was Romy. He was scowling. He was ugly. He was wearing an orange sweat suit and a black wig.

15

I kicked up as much ruckus as I could on the way back to the Riverbelle.

While Romy growled, cursed and dragged me along with my arm in a hammerlock, I kicked and yelled, and rekicked and reyelled. Not that I had much chance of getting away, but I wanted to slow him down as much as possible.

Every second I slowed him down brought help from Supergranny, Officer Inspect and the Coast Guard one second closer.

When we got to the Riverbelle, the scaffolding was already down and Remy was loading the floodlights on board.

He was shocked to see me and was in no mood for drop-in guests. For once, the smug, gloating look was wiped off his face.

The two of them pushed me up the gangplank and into the Grand Salon.

The poor Grand Salon.

You could hardly see the carpet for the pigs. In fact, it looked like a moving carpet of green-speckled gray pigs.

The corner with the buffet counter had been barricaded off from the pigs, and Romy and Remy pushed me over there, then threw me down against the wall.

"Where did YOU come from?" Remy demanded.

Oh, boy. Now what should I do? Keep my mouth shut? Tell them everything? Just give my name, rank and serial number like in old war movies? Even though I didn't *have* a rank and serial number?

Desperately, I tried to come up with a plan, a defense of some kind.

I could think of only two things, time and my mouth.

I had to buy time, and my mouth was my only weapon.

Maybe if I looked young and innocent enough and talked enough without really telling them anything, I could gain some time. I'd try to make them think I was *going* to tell them something any minute, if I could only get to the point.

The question was, could I make it work? My mouth, I mean. Could I make it open and have words come out? I tried the first word.

"Cleveland," I squeaked. "I came here from Cleveland."

They frowned identical frowns.

Quickly, I forged ahead. "But you probably mean where did I come from *today*. Because, of course, I live in town now. We moved here from Cleveland some time ago because my parents got new jobs here and —"

The frowns deepened. I figured I'd better circle a little closer to the point.

"But as to tonight, as to how I got here *tonight*, well, that was kind of an accident. I was out boating and water-skiing with some friends, and it was starting to get late, and I still hadn't had my turn to ski. I'm not much good at skiing, you see. I mean, I haven't skied much, so —"

"WHERE ARE THE REST OF THEM?" Romy shouted.

Rats. Another hope dashed. I'd hoped that somehow they wouldn't recognize me from that morning, wouldn't remember I was part of the Supergranny group. Granted, it was a long shot, but it *was* dark on the island.

Not dark enough, however. They knew exactly who I was.

I plowed on, looking as young and innocent as I could manage.

"Oh, you mean Supergranny. You mean, where is Supergranny. She's my neighbor. Of course, you may know her as Mrs. Oglepop. Most people call her Sadie Geraldine Oglepop, which is her real name.

"That little robot with her is her pet robot, Chesterton. He's slightly spoiled, actually. Although it would be better not to mention that to her. Now the hairy one, her name is Shackleford, and —"

"ARE THEY ON THE ISLAND?" Remy demanded.

On the island . . . that was an idea. Maybe if I could make them think Supergranny was on Magic Island, they would take time off to search it. And every minute they searched was a minute in our favor.

"Well, they might be," I said. "You see, I haven't seen them since we got separated waterskiing, but —"

"SHUT UP!" shouted Remy. "Tie him up! We've got to search the blasted island!"

They fell for it! It worked! Little fireworks of happiness exploded in my mind.

But the fireworks exploded too soon. Because just then another voice roared from the doorway: "WHAT'S GOING ON HERE?"

Another figure strode into the Grand Salon.

My mouth fell open in surprise. I forgot to look innocent. I forgot to look young. I forgot everything.

It was another one of them.

There was a third one. Chubby. Bald. 60ish. Still wearing bathing trunks and that weird mosquito netting. His name was Ritchie, he was the boss, and he was even meaner than Remy or Romy, if such a thing were possible.

No wonder Romy had seemed to get from the south end of the island back to the scaffolding so fast.

It wasn't Romy.

No wonder the Twittle twins had confounded police all these years. *There was an extra one nobody knew anything about.*

What a scam. Two of them could commit the crime while Twittle Three set up the perfect alibi. Two could hold up a jewelry store while the third sang in a church choir on TV. Two could rob a bank while the third faked a fainting spell in a crowded theater lobby.

That way, if somebody identified the crooks as the Twittle Twins, they could "prove" it wasn't by "proving" one of the twins had been singing in the church choir or fainting in the theater lobby at the time of the crime. They could claim the crooks *had* to be another set of twins, that it was a case of mistaken identity.

Clever. Fiendish. Cunning.

The Twittle Twins weren't twins at all. *They were the Twittle Triplets*.

At least, I hoped they were triplets. Heaven help the country if they were quads.

*   *   *   *   *   *

Unfortunately, Ritchie was too smart to fall for searching the island; he stopped the search cold.

"We're getting out of here in five minutes, and we're getting through that downriver lock in half an hour," he told the other two. "No buts, what ifs, or maybes. MOVE!"

Before I could mutter "You'll never get away with this" twenty times, he'd dragged me up to the pilot house, tied my hands behind me, then tied them to a leg of the table Clarence had moved up from the galley that morning.

Could it possibly have been that morning? It seemed 112 years ago.

At least there was one thing to be thankful for. The pilot house was just about the only spot on the Riverbelle that was hog-free. That was a small blessing.

All three Twittles were in the pilot house with me, getting ready to take the Riverbelle out of Magic Island and downriver. I could see their legs moving around from under the table.

I was mad. I was so mad I quit muttering and started shouting, "YOU'LL NEVER GET AWAY WITH THIS!"

The legs kept moving. One of the triplets was pouring

coffee into a thermos. Two of them were pulling their orange sweat suits back on over their bathing trunks.

"If you think the lockmaster will fall for this, you've got bananas in your brains," I yelled. "If you think you'll fool him just by painting the Riverbelle putrid green, you're nuts. He's been watching for the Riverbelle all day."

One of the triplets bent down and peered at me under the table. Romy had taken off his wig, they were all in their orange sweat suits, and I'd lost track of which was Remy, Romy or Ritchie.

Whichever one he was, he sat down cross-legged on the floor and smiled the ugliest smile ever smiled this century.

In one hand he held a plain, silver thermos. In the other he held a bottle of medicine.

He dangled them from his fingertips.

"Observe, my friend," he said.

Somehow, I could tell it was Ritchie. Maybe it was his voice. Maybe it was the extra-cocky way he had about him. Whatever it was, somehow I could tell.

"I can confide in you, young man, because you are going to be tied up under this table long after the Riverbelle is safely through the locks and on her way to New Orleans.

"See this thermos?" he asked.

I nodded slowly.

"It's *exactly* like the thermos the substitute lockmaster carries to work when he takes over during the lockmaster's vacation.

"Now, see this bottle?"

I nodded again.

"It's sleeping pills, young man. Now, watch closely."

83

He set the thermos on the floor and opened the bottle of sleeping pills. He poured several pills into the steaming thermos, closed it tightly, and shook it. All the time, he smiled that fiendish smile.

"One minute from now I'll leave the Riverbelle, my dear young friend," he said. "I'll take a skiff to shore, and pick up my motorcycle, hidden a few steps from the bank. I'll hop on it and be at the lock before the Riverbelle is midchannel.

"Then I'll drop in on my good friend, the substitute lockmaster, who's on duty tonight. I made a point of meeting him last week at the county fair. Just sat down next to him at the hog judging and started talking about hogs. Told him I'm a New York mystery writer doing a book set on the Mississippi River."

Ritchie cackled.

"He fell for it. Said he would be delighted to help with my research. Tonight I'll just happen to drop in during his coffee break at the lock to ask a few questions about river lore. When he gets carried away explaining, I'll switch the thermoses.

"He'll be snoozing like a baby by the time the Riverbelle reaches the locks."

Ritchie leaned forward and whispered.

"Then I, my good young man, will open the locks, hop aboard, and New Orleans, here we come — with a million-dollar boat and $30,000 worth of the finest hogs in America!"

I·kicked at the thermos, but missed.

He grabbed it and laughed. He was still laughing as he left the pilot house. Still laughing as he climbed down to the lower deck, then down the ladder to the runabout. Still laughing until the outboard motor on his skiff drowned out the sound.

The Riverbelle's engine thumped alive and began to purr. Romy was at the helm and Remy was down below, guiding him out of Pirate's Pond. I could hear his voice crackling to Romy over a walkie-talkie.

Slowly, we moved. In five minutes we had slipped out of the shelter of Magic Island and into the dark Mississippi.

Quietly, I lay down on my back and scooted as far as I could to the outer edge of the table. I could see Romy at the wheel and black sky and water out a corner of the window.

The blinding white light of a barge coming upriver swept the water.

I hoped against hope that the barge would see us and stop us. But we passed it silently in the night.

Where was Supergranny? Angela and Vannie? Officer Inspect and the Coast Guard?

Were they out there waiting? Watching us?

How could I warn them about Ritchie drugging the lock-master? Warn them that there *was* a Ritchie? That the Twittles were triplets?

The miserable truth was that I couldn't warn them. I was trapped. It was out of my hands.

"Hurry, Supergranny," I whispered. "Hurry."

16

The Riverbelle slipped quietly through the night.

Both Romy and Remy were in the pilot house now, cackling and congratulating each other on their perfect crime.

On top of all my other worries, I worried that they would run aground or crash into one of the old-fashioned wing dams left along the shore from earlier days of river travel.

But they didn't.

Somewhere they had learned to pilot large boats. And despite their goofing off, they paid strict attention to their own copy of the navigation charts.

So somehow we managed to stay in the channel.

They more or less seemed to have forgotten about me, and I stayed as quiet as possible so as not to remind them.

I even pretended to sleep, hoping they'd drop their guard. I didn't know exactly what I'd do after their guard was dropped, but, who knows? Maybe something. Hope springs eternal.

All too soon, we reached the downriver lock.

It's sort of a water elevator that would take the Riverbelle from high water on one side of the dam to low water on the other.

It worked this way: Gates on one side of the lock would open, the Riverbelle would go inside, then the gates would close. The water level in the "elevator" would go down, down, down, and the Riverbelle would go down, down, down with it. Finally the water would get down to the level on the other side of the dam. Then the gates on the opposite end of the lock would open, and the Riverbelle would go out.

It was like going over a cliff the easy way.

Of course, it worked the other way around, too. I mean, boats going upriver would be *raised* to the water level on the other side of the dam.

Romy lined up with the lock and blasted the Riverbelle's whistle, the signal that he wanted to go through the lock.

The whistle blared so loud it shook the floor and made my table jump.

We waited.

Had Ritchie drugged the substitute lockmaster? Would Ritchie open the lock himself?

I strained as far out from under the table as I could, desperate to see what was going on.

We waited.

Suddenly, Romy and Remy began to laugh and talk excitedly.

"There he is," Romy said.

"Yup, there's Ritchie," Remy said gleefully.

"He's giving the signal," Romy chirped.

"New Orleans, here we come," Remy sang.

Slowly, the lock gates opened. Slowly, we moved inside. Slowly, the gates closed behind us.

Any minute the water level would go down. Any minute I would feel the Riverbelle going down with it.

But nothing happened.

We waited.

Nothing happened.

"Romy," Ritchie's voice called from the lock wall. "Come down here a minute."

"He wants you," Remy said.

Romy went out on the top deck, which was almost level with the lock wall. I saw his legs swing over the railing, then walk along the wall.

There was a commotion on the wall, a commotion of strange noises and glimpses of arms flying in several directions. Remy ducked to the floor out of sight from the window.

"JOSHUA," a voice called. "It's all over, Joshua. We've got them both." It was Officer Inspect.

"We've got both of them, Joshua, where are you?" another voice called. It was Supergranny.

I closed my eyes. I felt Remy glancing in my direction. If only I could convince him I was asleep.

I could hear him creeping along the floor.

How could I let Officer Inspect and Supergranny know

they *didn't* have all the Twittles? That it *wasn't* over?

I opened one eye. Remy was gone. What would he do? Escape? Sneak behind them and take them by surprise?

I shivered, remembering the gun Remy had held on Clyde the Crazy Calliope that morning.

Would Remy come back and use me as a hostage?

I was surprised he hadn't thought of that already. Somehow I knew he *would* think of it, that any second he would be back.

I had to do something.

Desperately, I scooted toward the pilot house's open doorway, dragging the table with me. Luckily, the Riverbelle was listing slightly to port. That helped, because the table and I were going somewhat downhill. I wedged the table across the doorway and began to shout.

"TRIPLETS," I shouted at top volume. "THE TWIT-TLES ARE TRIPLETS! GET THE THIRD ONE! TRIPLETS!!!"

That did it. All at once it dawned on Remy that I was his ticket out of this mess. Here he came at a gallop. Too late, he saw the table blocking his path.

"UGUPHUHHUPP," he gasped, as he crashed into the table, slid across it on his belly, and rolled against the opposite wall.

Something big and hairy streaked over the table after him, barking furiously.

Something small and quick streaked under the table and grabbed him by the ankle.

Kallummp-kallummpup, kallummp-kallummpup, kallummp-kallummpup — three more runners hurdled the table.

89

Each kallummp-kallummpup made the table jump and jerked my arms, which were tied to its leg, but I didn't mind. It was Supergranny, Angela and Vannie, and it was the best *kallummp-kallummpupping* I'd ever heard.

Remy didn't know what hit him.

From under my table I could see him cowering in the corner as Shackleford growled and Chesterton gripped his ankle. Angela and Vannie held his arms behind him while Supergranny tied his wrists with her special strength grosgrain ribbon.

I had to laugh. It was the second time today a Twittle had been wrapped up with Plan 432B. And no crooks in the world deserved it more.

"Joshua, where are you?" Angela called as they finished wrapping up Remy.

I scooted partway out from under the table and looked up at them.

"Good evening, Ladies and Chesterton," I said. "Congratulations on a beautiful job."

17

You'd think the ride upriver that night would have been happy.

And, at first, it was.

After all, we had the Riverbelle back and the Twittles were headed for jail. At first, we felt flooded with relief and happiness.

And, of course, there was so much to tell.

"It was a trap," Vannie explained. "A lock trap for the Twittles."

As soon as they got my signal that the Riverbelle was on Magic Island, they had moved out of earshot and radioed Officer Inspect.

Unknown to me, the police and Coast Guard were watching us from the minute the Riverbelle inched out of Magic Island.

"Remember that upriver barge?" Angela asked.

I nodded.

"Packed with police," she said.

Meanwhile, our Supergranny group and the entire River-belle crew, including Mazie, had hidden with Officer Inspect at the lock.

Supergranny sketched a composite drawing of Romy and Remy, and the substitute lockmaster identified him as the mystery writer he had met at the county fair.

Of course, he wasn't really Romy or Remy anymore than he was a New York mystery writer. He was Ritchie: Twittle Three.

But the point was, he was a Twittle, a crook, and they were ready for him.

When Ritchie arrived at the lock with the drugged coffee, Officer Inspect arrested him.

"When Ritchie went out on the lock wall to open the gates, two police officers hid in the shadows, giving him orders," Supergranny said.

"Thank heavens Joshua figured out the Twittles were triplets and not twins," Captain said as she steered the Riverbelle back out of the lock and headed upriver. "Otherwise Remy might have sneaked up behind us and retaken the Riverbelle."

I appreciated what she said, but there hadn't been much figuring out to it. Once the three of them were standing together looking identical, any fence post could have figured out they weren't just twins.

"They wanted to pull the perfect double crime," Supergranny said. "Their idea was to rustle the pigs in the fog, then steal the Riverbelle for their getaway. They planned to sell everything to a New Orleans fence for stolen goods . . ."

". . . And live like triple kings in Brazil," Vannie finished.

The Twittles had holed up in a downtown hotel for weeks, waiting for the right foggy weather. It was their bad luck that the fog hit the same day as ROTRATTT. How could they steal a boat loaded with 800 bikers? They tried to scare Captain from transporting the bikers, but that didn't work. So they decided to take over the Riverbelle mid-channel after the bikers unloaded.

It had almost worked.

*   *   *   *   *   *

We stopped once on our way upriver to unload the hogs at the Riverdale Farm dock.

Farmer Riverdale and his family were out in force, clear down to the youngest grandchild, three Des Moines cousins and a niece playing "Bugler's Holiday" on her trumpet.

They were totally thrilled to get the hogs back, and never mind the green speckles.

"We've got the hoses and scrub brushes at the ready back in the confinement shed," Farmer Riverdale told us. "We're going to have these hogs de-speckled by morning if it takes all night."

It took the Riverdales some time to round up the hogs and herd them down the gangplank. We helped all we could, but it wasn't easy because the Riverbelle had so many nooks and crannies for the hogs to hide in or get stuck in by mistake.

93

At one point, when we thought we had them all off, three more turned up under the sink in the galley.

Finally we got them all unloaded and watched them trundling across the field in the night, herded toward their shed by all shapes, sizes and ages of Riverdales.

I guess it was about the time the last hog made its exit that our elation ebbed and reality moved in.

The truth was, the Riverbelle was a disaster.

Picture putrid green paint sprayed everywhere, even on the windows. Picture straw and hog poop ankle-deep in places. Picture shredded banners, torn drapes and broken deck chairs.

And where the Twittles hadn't sprayed green paint, the hogs had tracked it, including all over the carpet in the Grand Salon.

I mean, the Riverbelle was a 40-million-times-bigger mess than Vannie's room at its worst. I mean it made Vannie's room look as neat as the Marine Corp Band passing in parade review.

Supergranny, Angela, Vannie and I found four reasonably undamaged deck chairs and sat down on the top deck in darkness.

It was like sitting on an abandoned battlefield.

Up in the pilot house, the solemn Captain was at the wheel. Second Mate stood loyally beside her. Clarence stood at the prow, staring into the night, too discouraged even to think of cards.

Up on Clyde the Crazy Calliope's platform, Mazie played "I'm So Lonesome I Could Cry." The mournful sounds drifted through the cool, dark river air. Now and then a farmhouse light blinked from shore.

Supergranny shook her head sadly.

"You might as well know the facts," she said in a low voice. "Even if Captain's insurance pays for most of the damages, the repairs will take the rest of the summer. And she can't afford to stop running the Riverbelle that long. She needs the money from ticket sales to make the loan payments on the Riverbelle.

"I'm afraid if she shuts down that long she will go bankrupt and lose the Riverbelle after all."

Bankrupt!

Lose the Riverbelle!

After all we had done to get the Riverbelle back!

It wasn't fair.

I thought of Captain working thirty years on river barges to save money for the Riverbelle's down payment.

I thought of how she spent every winter tuning its engine, repainting, and cleaning its carpet and drapes.

I thought of how proud she had been that morning. Of the gaily colored flags and balloons. Of how much pleasure the Riverbelle gave people in our town.

All of it gone for nothing. All because the greedy Twittle Twerps wanted to live like kings in Brazil.

"Couldn't we help?" Vannie asked wearily. "I mean, Farmer Riverdale's family gathered around to redo the pigs. Couldn't we gather around to redo the Riverbelle?"

"We could repaint," I said.

"We could clean carpets," Angela said.

Supergranny smiled. "It's a good thought, but we just couldn't do it fast enough. It would take a miracle, a thousand hands, a —"

Suddenly she stopped. She stared at the Mississippi. Then she grabbed her purse and rummaged through it for her address book.

She turned the pages quickly. "Radcliff, Reed, Robertson — here it is — ROTRATTT General Chairman — 555-0001."

She jumped up so fast, she dropped her purse and we had to scramble around gathering up all her stuff before it rolled into the river.

"CLARENCE," she yelled. "Help me place a phone call through that ship-to-shore radio."

"Cross your fingers," she yelled back at us over her shoulder, "and hope we can stir up a miracle!"

18

By the time we reached the Riverbelle dock, it was teeming with ROTRATTT bikers, this time without their bikes.

No sooner had we tied up than they thundered up the gangplank. In platoons.

The ROTRATTT General Chairman came first, carrying a clipboard and wearing jeans, a ROTRATTT sweat-shirt, tennis shoes and a portable microphone.

Our parents came next, loaded down with sleeping bags. They hugged and kissed us and laughed and congratulated the Captain on getting the Riverbelle back.

The ROTRATTT bikers had returned!

They were going to restore the Riverbelle, and Mom was there to report it for her newspaper.

"We knew you all would be exhausted, so we brought

sleeping bags. You can nap while I work on my story and Dad works his shift," Mom said.

"I'm on the 10 p.m. to midnight sandwich-and-coffee-making shift for the carpenter and paint crews," Dad explained.

One thousand bikers had been divided into platoons and shifts by the ROTRATTT General Chairman. The carpenters, painters, professional carpet cleaners, furniture refinishers, window washers and seamstresses would do the actual restoring.

The lawyers, doctors, housewives, househusbands, bankers, teachers, poets, actors and everybody else would do backup and supply.

For instance, one backup group formed a long chain to pass the deck chairs down to the dock to be repaired. Another long chain passed cleaning and painting supplies up.

Out on the dock, electricians were rigging up floodlights so everybody could see what they were doing. In five minutes the dock, the Riverbelle and half the river were lit up, bright as noon.

One end of the dock was lined with rows of industrial sewing machines, already humming away, repairing drapes and making new flags and banners.

All across town, sleepy storekeepers had opened yard-good stores and paint shops to provide supplies.

Meanwhile, gofers with trucks and station wagons lined the dock road, ready to make supply runs.

A bright yellow cook tent had been set up near the gangplank to keep everybody's strength up with food and coffee. And the entire Riverview bakery had been transformed into a baby-sitting service for the workers' children.

The ROTRATTT General Chairman stood by the pilot house, surveying it all through binoculars, and giving orders and cheering on the troops over her microphone.

Supergranny, Angela, Vannie and I put Shackleford and Chesterton in the pilot house and walked around shaking our heads in disbelief. Supergranny had stirred up the miracle with her call to the ROTRATTT General Chairman, but even she couldn't believe it.

"All this talent. All this good will. All this practical horse sense. It's a miracle," she kept saying.

At first we thought Mom had been silly to bring our sleeping bags. How could we sleep with all this excitement?

But pretty soon the work settled down to a steady roar, and there wasn't much new to watch — just more of what we had already seen, and lots of it.

Captain and Second Mate still roamed the decks blissfully, but Mazie finally gave up and went over to the Captain's penthouse for a snooze.

Clarence, of course, parked himself at the recreation area where people took breaks between shifts. They played Frisbee, Trivial Pursuit and cards, cards, cards. Clarence was in his glory. He sat down on an old crate for an all-night card game.

Finally, Supergranny, Angela, Vannie and I went back up to the pilot house.

It was the only spot not damaged in the heist, and it was cozy to stretch out in our sleeping bags with the sounds of work going on around us.

Shackleford and Chesterton slept peacefully under my

former table, and Supergranny sat against the wall in her sleeping bag, knitting.

She was knitting Ferrari-red booties for her newborn great niece in Heidelberg, West Germany. She had just gotten a call about the baby the week before.

"What do you think was the best part of all?" Supergranny asked as her needles clicked along.

"The Captain reboarding the Riverbelle at the lock," Angela suggested.

"The Twittle Twerps going to jail," Vannie suggested.

"It sure *wasn't* falling into the nest of snakes," I suggested.

Everybody laughed, then we settled down to sleep.

While we slept, camera crews from all the major television networks, plus cable and PBS, swooped in to cover the bikers at work. People around the world watched the Riverbelle restored right on television, and the next day Mom's newspaper story was picked up by The Associated Press and by the International Herald Tribune in Paris.

And when we awoke the next morning and stepped out into the bright summer sunshine, there was Captain, once again inspecting her beautiful old sternwheeler.

Once again, the Riverbelle looked as fancy as a floating wedding cake — if they make red and white wedding cakes. Once again, banners flew from gaily colored smokestacks, balloons danced from curved railings, and layers on layers of decks reached to the sky.

Just then Mazie and Clyde the Crazy Calliope broke into "America the Beautiful," and a thousand worn-out but happy bikers sang along.

And I knew that NOW, this moment, was the best part of all.

Then it was time to head home.

Captain gave us hugs all around, with extra hugs for Shackleford. Then she gave us hugs all around again.

Mom took our car home, and Dad, who had wound up working three sandwich-and-coffee-making shifts, took the Ferrari and ski boat back to Supergranny's.

The rest of us climbed into the helicopter.

We lifted into the air and saluted the Captain, who was waving to us from the Riverbelle. Then we started home above the sparkling Mississippi.

"By the way, they named my niece 'Sadie' after me," Supergranny shouted above the whirring of the propellers. "I sure would like to see her. After we rest a few days, what do you think your parents would say about your taking a little trip to Germany?

"It would be fun seeing my baby niece.

"And it would be fun showing you Europe. There is always something interesting to do in Europe."

ABOUT THE AUTHOR

Beverly Van Hook grew up in Huntington, West Virginia, graduated from Ohio University, Athens, and now lives in Charlottesville, Virginia and Chicago, Illinois. A journalist who wrote for national magazines before turning to fiction, she has received numerous writing awards, including the Cornelia Meigs Award for Children's Literature and the Isabel Bloom Award for the Arts. She is married to an advertising executive and has three children and an Old English sheepdog exactly like Shackleford.

ABOUT THE ARTIST

Catherine Wayson grew up in Iowa and now lives in Huntsville, Alabama, where she is a full-time professional illustrator and free-lance artist and photographer. Her paintings and photographs have appeared in juried shows nationally and throughout the Midwest.